Asa's Blessing

Book Two of Vade Mecum

#16/50 DHD

To Jonny! Enjoy! DHD

By D.H. Dhaenens

Flammable Penguins Publishing

Table of Contents

First published in Great Britain in 2018
by FLAMMABLE PENGUINS PUBLISHING

ISBN 978-0-9956967-0-9

FLAMMABLE PENGUINS PUBLISHING
International House
24 Holborn Viaduct
CITY OF LONDON
London EC1A 2BN

www.flammablepenguins.com

To Claire, my shining star

Andie, thank you for being a friend

You've helped this come together

Kat - you can stop poking me, it's done

Chapter 1

G

Despite ringing the door at the street level, Gabrielle was ushered in on the second level of the house as Etta opened the door.

"Gabrielle! What a lovely surprise!" Henrietta pulled the younger and taller woman into a hug.

"Oh come in, come in. You should have called ahead! I look terrible." She primped up her white curls a bit, though they were immaculately caught in a low bun.

"Nonsense, Etta, you look wonderful." Gabrielle smiled. "And I like keeping my visits surprises. I don't like having things to look forward to."

"I do, sweet girl." With the help of her cane, Etta retreated to her rocking chair and motioned to the old fashioned love seat. "There's some soda in the kitchen, I keep it for the youngsters like you. There's also beer."

Gabrielle chuckled and sat down in the love seat. "Thank you." She said. "But I didn't come merely to socialise." She looked around.

"You would be so much more comfortable in the Scribe's building, Etta. The new one is so modern! It has trash chutes on every floor and marble countertops."
"Oh honey, I'm not long for this world. It doesn't matter where I sit when I look out my window."
"I suppose not." Gabrielle took a deep breath. "I'll help myself to a beer if you don't mind."
"Get me one as well. Ethan doesn't like it when I drink but I dislike drinking alone." The old lady flashed only half a mouth's worth of teeth as she smiled.
"He's your son, he's meant to look out for you." Said Gabrielle.

Nevertheless, she grabbed a beer for the old mage and one for herself.
"Speaking of men, where's Furcifer?" Asked the old lady.
"He's... oh I suppose I can tell you." A bit of faux confidentiality never hurt a dialogue, and the upcoming conversation was not one she was keen to have.
"He's working on identifying factions to have talks with about the laws." Gabrielle said as she sat down with the beers.
"The International Mage Guild in particular is not very responsive. It looks like they're quite busy with something." She glanced at the lady, wondering if she could put two and two together.
"Someone found the first notebook, Etta." She said as she

popped the cap off and put the beer down.

The old woman's hand hovered over the beer before clasping it and swishing back a large gulp.

"You know how keen they are about bringing back Redford from –"

"I thought that nonsense was gone and buried." Etta interrupted the other mage.

"So did we. We hoped that you'd taken care in getting rid of it." Gabrielle's tone turned somewhat disapproving.

"Remember who you are talking to, child. I predate your entire organisation."

"My organisation will outlive you." She sipped her beer daintily. "But I'll mind my tone."

That bit of goodwill did not seem enough to placate Etta.

"So you come to me to ask where the rest of them are, is that it?"

"I have the authority to extract that information from you." She swirled a finger. Small magical particles floated down.

Etta sipped her beer again.

"You cannot get that information from me, honey." Etta smiled sweetly, suppressing a beer burp.

"I have safeguards in place to keep such information safe. You remember the seventies. Plenty of dæmons around from that trend of trying to summon ghosts. It turns out that making yourself possession proof keeps you from being influenced by all sorts of spells which aim to take over your personality."

Gabrielle hissed. She was right. The old guard had a crude but effective system to guard against demonic, and other, kinds of possession.

Much like a hard drive, a human mind could be partitioned. With hard work and perseverance, one could create a secondary personality, which would trap any dæmon within the first personality and take over control. It meant a possessed mage could find help to expel the dæmon without doing any harm. This technique was now frowned upon and deemed too dangerous, but many mages alive in the seventies still had such safeguards in place. Threatening an octogenarian who had a lifetime of experience under her belt would not do her any good.

"I'm merely asking for your help in this, Etta." She smiled a little, hoping to soften up the woman.

Etta's eyes wandered to a picture of her and a young man. A chubby form with a sweet face, light brown hair and a slightly freckled face... Gabrielle followed her gaze and looked over.

"He's safe, Etta." She said.

"No thanks to you, missy."
At that point, Gabrielle knew she had lost her. She looked at the picture again.
What made her frown was not the simple frame the picture was in, so very different from the ornate photo frames around her. It was the fact it had been taken in this room, but with the new wallpaper that had been hung up less than a month ago. Just before the notebook had been recovered. Gabrielle felt a chill as it clicked.
"You..." She got up and gasped. "You gave it to him?"

"There comes a time we have to take responsibility for what we did, Gabrielle. Four of us already did that night. I will not be long in following them. What that boy does will determine his fate and that of your little magic world." She got up with a fierceness Gabrielle had rarely seen in the usually sedate old lady. "I just pray I gave him enough head start to find all of it. You know just as well as me that's why the IMG is suddenly so busy - they're trying to track him down, but he could bring them down."

"In fact, he might just bring all of you down, and your elitist factions. I know he'll do the right thing, though. Oh honey I'm tired. You're welcome to take your beer." She ushered Gabrielle towards the door before uttering a last warning, which made Gabrielle shiver.

"But, Gabrielle. Beware. You should leave Twitch to deal with that spell. It's done enough damage."

Chapter 2

Gabrielle walked through the parking area near Etta's house. It was beautiful - the car park was separated from the grove by a lovely little park, but she was in no mindset to enjoy it right now. With shaky hands, she lit a cigarette and then marched back towards her car. She hadn't smoked in years, and chuckled nervously when she realised she had magicked the cigarettes out of thin air. It was hard to quit smoking when you could just intuitively summon a pack of smokes. And it seemed her hands had not forgotten that automatic movement.

She briefly wondered about what Etta had said.

He'll do the right thing, though.

Right now, she wasn't even sure what that meant anymore. Her trembling hands moved to grasp the cigarette, then touched it again, before she decided to take her phone out. She had left it turned off for the entire visit so there had been no distractions. She knew at least one mage who could not go even a minute without attention. The phone beeped and started up.

Today had started with a simple assignment. Visit Henrietta and try to find the whereabouts of the journals before any more of them were found. Clearly, the woman had no intention of cooperating. Her son Ethan was part of the IMG, but he knew nothing about the location of the notebooks. The man had given up the notes and the letters his mother had written to the faction, but they were vague and not very informative. Unless he was holding more back. It didn't matter. He was out of their reach as long as he belonged to another faction. They could be very effective safe havens.

At this point, there might only be one person who knew where the journals were and that person happened to be the sole person she had ever tortured. Back then she'd hardly known who he was. He had just been some boy, someone who stood in her way.

The Spell had come about somewhere in the late sixties, before any real faction had been created. The Scribes were the only group doing anything of any relevance in the magic community. Even though they were the only faction, they had been a ragtag group of about ten people trying to organise themselves and the spells they knew into a compendium, with plans to expand this publication every year, much like a dictionary. These were the first published spellbooks, a secret of the magic community - only recently had non-mages learned just how far back the modern history of magic went.

Any spell was to be accepted into the compendium. It was a time for experimentation, discovery. The spell Etta and six other mages had created, however, was so different and dangerous the magic community as a whole recoiled from it.
They had been warned that expulsion would be their fate, and they proceeded anyway. Back then there was no safety net whatsoever for anyone breaking the rules and getting hurt in doing so.

She stared up at the sky. Right now it was clear who had found the first notebook. The notebook was important - parts of the Spell Etta and her conspirators had performed had been written down in many different notebooks, hidden among other spells.

Recently, a rival faction had shown interest in finding the Spell, reaching out to mages who did not belong to any faction to aid them in finding the parts required to puzzle it back together. It would be a disaster for any faction to see this spell resurface. Gabrielle had been trying to bury the news, hoping to make sure nobody was going to try and find it. If Twitch was out there, he would have received the message and would know that it was no longer safe.

She flicked the cigarette into a bin and got into the car. The notifications had started streaming in on her phone. One was an invoice email with a photo attachment. She raised an eyebrow, thumb fluttering over the attached image, before deciding to download it.
It was a tasteful boudoir picture of a man stretched out on a vintage chaise longue. A shock of bright red hair, ice blue eyes staring defiantly into the camera. Down from there, a somewhat defined torso with light golden skin, and a small patch of bright red pubic hair, the rest mercifully hidden under a strategically placed silk scarf.

"Oh for fu-"

Chapter 3

Twitch loved fantasy books. The ones where mages fought epic evil beings and got lost in forests. What irked him, however, was that they never seemed to have any real jobs. To keep being able to add to his collection of wands and fantasy paperbacks, he had a job.

Magic had recently made a return to his life and he was not sure how to feel about that. Of course he still used magic, magic had never really left his life, he supposed. But there were no magic stores here. There were not even any magic users that he was aware of, so it was just a thing he used to reach high shelves in his house. In fact it had been nice to spend some time with two other people who had powers like his, but right now he was just getting back to reality.

The school bell rang, reminding him it was time to get to work. "Right..." He straightened up and made his way to the classroom.
He taught sixteen and seventeen year olds, college grade. They were usually pretty good, a little unruly but smart. They were ambitious and boisterous, if somewhat uninterested in history.

He turned to walk to class when suddenly, he felt someone bump into him.
"Oh! You're back!" Lydia grinned as she looked up to him, strawberry blond curls bouncing. She was the college level maths teacher, and a good friend, for someone he'd met at work. He liked her - she had an open face and was easy to talk to.
"Ah! Hi Lydia... Yeah I got back last night." He smiled. He'd missed a few days of teaching to go visit Henrietta. Luckily, there were plenty of eager interns who didn't mind short notice periods.
"Glad you're back. One of the interns messed up the Napoleonic period. The entire class flunked the test you made, so they're still looking into how they're fixing this... Maybe a catch up lesson on Friday if you are up for that?"
"Sure thing. With the A-levels coming up I don't want them to learn the wrong thing... When's the mock A-levels?" He asked, looking around for the notice board.

"In a few weeks. You've got time to undo the damage." She smiled as she walked with him. "You seem different."

"Really?" He raised an eyebrow and opened the door to his class. Perhaps he'd dressed much more casual than he had thought. He usually wore nothing less than a dress shirt with tie and a blazer. Today however, he had rushed out in a t-shirt with a jacket over it.

"It's okay right? I mean I know the principal is a stickler for his teachers looking good..." He fussed with the hem of the shirt.

"Stop that. You look good." She grinned and playfully tapped his hand. "It's a good look on you." She decided with a nod.

"No, I mean you seem... different." She shrugged and hesitated.

There was a momentary tension, in which he could feel a little more than just usual social interaction. Something magical, perhaps.

"See you later. We should do lunch later." She turned away and rushed to the teacher's lounge to prepare for her class before he could react.

"Holding you to that!" He answered. Maybe it had been the time away but he felt a little more.... Empowered. Self confident.

She turned around to wave before vanishing. He shook his head and walked into the classroom.

Twitch sighed as he prepared for class. She was a friend but even so she didn't know a thing about what he really did. His magic, where he had come from, why he had so many herbs in his house and why he wore little beads and charms around his neck and wrists. Even if he no longer needed it, he had kept some of Aiden's commuter beads. It was a nice link back to Zeus City, and out here they were nigh irreplaceable. He was nowhere near crafty enough to work with boiling glass and magic right now, but he was getting somewhere in making his own candles with spells in them. It was quite the different method - he wrote spells on the wick then made them into thick strands which he put in the middle of the wax. Now he just had to work on actually using them without freaking out about the thick flame the wicks produced.

As the pupils streamed in, he rolled his head in his neck and sighed. It was time to straighten them out.

"Good to see you again kids. I hear you covered Napoleon while I was out?"

"Yeees, siiir." The class echoed at him.

"Wonderful, that's one of my favourite eras!"

"You say that about all the periods... Sir!" One of the boys interjected.

"Maybe." He looked over with a smile. "Ah, Derek. Please stand up and tell me what you know about Napoleon."

"Uh." The loudmouth boy stood up and spied around, hoping

someone had their book open. Some pupils just closed it with a little chuckle.
"Uuuh... He was French? And there's this artist called Napoleon Dynamite!"
"And I was worried I would have to unteach you guys a bunch before getting to the good stuff. Thanks, Derek. That is correct. He was indeed French." He chuckled. He was always careful when putting his students on the spot - he didn't want them to become so shy they would never bother trying to reply to his questions.
Derek thankfully sat down and shoved the boy next to him, who'd closed his book when he had been called upon so he couldn't peek.

The hour flew by. He was just about through the first half of the chapter when the bell rang and the students got up
"Alright, please read the rest of the chapter before Thursday's class!" He called out as another class moved past them, merging into a large stream going through the halls. Now he had an hour to decide what to do about the lesson plan - he'd hoped to be post Napoleon by now so he had to bump up everything. If he just stopped at World War II and did not teach any post 1945 history, he could probably still finish in time. As he thought he gathered up his things. As he put the lesson plan away he spotted the notebook in his bag.

He had started this without any help from anyone. He was usually such a pack animal, someone who'd always lived in a community. To tackle a problem this big on his own... He had to admit he'd been tempted more than once to just pick up the phone and call Furcifer. But he wasn't sure Furcifer was on his side anymore. He'd very much stuck to one way communication, letting Furcifer know just about where he was and that he was still alive. But that was it.

He looked up, hearing someone clear their throats. Lydia was standing in the doorway, looking over him with her arms crossed.

"Lunch, Asa. Come on." The principal insisted they didn't use nicknames for one another, so the kids would respect them or some bull. He guessed it worked when you didn't have a first name from the sixteenth century.

"It's lunch already? Oh dear." He got up and put away the last of his books.

"Thanks. I was getting lost in my own work there." He smiled a little as he got up. "You want to just go to the canteen?"

"Yeah, I'm not leaving the building." She nodded. "I've been feeling a bit under the weather." She added quickly.

Twitch looked over to her, worried. "Hope you're not coming down with anything."

"Oh you know how it is. Kids get sick all the time." She smiled a little and pushed some hair back into her hair bun.

"Well, let's get you some nutritional, state funded... Chicken nuggets." He chuckled as he read the menu. "Sounds ok to me."

"Still better than a sandwich and crisps." Lydia picked up a tray and handed one over to Twitch.

"So what did you get up to while you were off?"

"A family matter. My great aunt needed some help with something." Twitch said as he was handed a plate of food. "Nothing world changing."

"I never know with you." She teased and turned to head for the desserts. "For all I know you're with MI5."

Her energy was electric, and it was contagious. He felt himself cheer up just being around her. Again, it seemed to be more than just good humour and a sparkling personality.

"I would love to tell you but I'd have to shoot you." He followed her with a little grin. "But I'd be the worst secret agent ever."

"Well, they always say it's the guy who looks least like James Bond." She said. She held a pudding cup in one hand and a pot of fruit salad in the other. After a moment she put back the fruit salad and set the pudding cup on her tray.

"I'm totally a James Bond type!" Twitch picked up an orange and added it to his tray. "Let's see if we can find a spot away from the teens." He walked away from the lunch line and looked around.

"They're young adults, Asa." She teased and walked towards the tables, suddenly shivering. For a second Twitch felt a strange magic in the air. Wild, unkempt.

"Here's fine." She slammed her tray down on the nearest table and demonstratively sat down. Her nuggets hovered a split second, then crashed down onto her plate. It was almost cartoonish. She picked up her knife and fork like nothing had happened, dodging Twitch's looks as he sat down across from her.

Twitch had clearly felt it - there had been a sudden surge of magic, a definite feel of something. This time he was sure. He had seen the hovering and it had not been his magic. The feel of magic had been so localised he doubted it was anyone else. Plus, she was definitely acting suspiciously.

"Well, enjoy!" She chimed cheerily, trying to dispel the worried looks she was getting from her colleague.

"Are you sure you're o-"

"How's that Napoleonic rehash going?" She furiously speared a chicken nugget, seemingly angry at its defiance of gravity earlier.

"Oh! Yes." He got the hint. "It seems that most of them not remembering what I teach them for longer than ten minutes might be working in my favour. I got through half the chapter today and I'll be finishing it up on Thursday, hopefully I can give them a pop quiz then. Perhaps I'll just prepare one for the first half of the chapter just in case." He nodded. "How about you? You think you can get them ready for the mock A-levels?" She seemed unwilling to talk to it so he dropped it. Perhaps a school setting was not the best place for this either way.

"Oh you forget I'm good at my job. I've been having them rehash all week." She smiled and picked up some mash. "I'm hoping they all get top grades for this one."
"Shouldn't be hard, you have been coaching them well. They pretty much expect to be tested every time so they sure study more than my students."

He had to admire her strict way of working - she took the job very seriously. At least more serious than he did. To him, this felt like a way to pay the rent more than anything. She had a passion.
"Anyway. Would you like to come over to mine tonight?" Twitch looked over. They usually hung out together when they had little to do, and he could tell something was off. Maybe

she would feel better talking about it when she was not at work.

Lydia looked over to him for a few seconds before nodding. "Sure. That sounds like fun." She said.

Twitch nodded. Whatever it was, he hoped she could just open up to him about it. He had to admit, the idea that a friend he got along with could have magic was exciting. Dispelling the thought he picked up another chicken nugget and ate it.

Chapter 4

An ocean away, Furcifer was staring out the window of his office on the top floor of the Elite headquarters. It had been a long day and it didn't seem like it would be ending soon. This call had been dragging on for an hour and while he'd been on the phone he could feel his phone vibrate every time a new message came in.

"Mmm. Sure. Get them to draw up an approval plan for this and I'll review it. Of course I'll give it my utmost attention." He promised, though he had forgotten the name of the person on the other end of the phone by now. But he was starting to dislike them.

"Yes, of course. Reducing caffeine abuse is... important." He made a face and threw back the last of the espresso he had been holding. "I will be happy to look at it. Goodnight." He could hear the door open. He knew only one person would come into his office without knocking.

Furcifer put the cup down as Gabrielle entered. He could smell smoke on her which was never a good sign. For her not to have complete control of the situation was scary. She marched in on high heels, wearing chain mail and commuter beads at all times. You did not want to get into a fight with her. Her shining silver hair was tied away into a loose low tail and it seemed like she had taken the time to do her make up today. He could notice some highlighter on her strong cheekbones and a definite attempt to define her eyebrows. She was not a conventional beauty - her features were a bit too strong for that - but she carried herself with a grace and authority that made people notice her.

"Bad news?" She asked him airily.
"This call? Not at all." He shook his head then checked his phone, raising an eyebrow as he scrolled through the deluge of emails that had come in during his call.

"Turns out the IMG's leader didn't like my present." He shrugged. The messages were from several officials in the International Mage Guild but the gist of the communications was the same. Somewhat outraged.
"You sent him flowers with a nude picture of yourself." Gabrielle pinched the bridge of her nose.
"I had to get his attention somehow."

"Honestly, Furcifer, you're the first one I know to use dick pics in negotiations."
"It was not a dick pic! It was a nice boudoir style photo with soft lensing and everything. Well, you'll see the details on the bill I left on your desk."
I at least want a print of that if I'm going to pay for it." She pointed a finger.
"I spoke to Henrietta."

"So the first notebook has been uncovered." Furcifer extrapolated after a moment's silence. That was what she was most known for - the Spell. After she used it she had hidden it, very carefully. It was said only she knew where it was.
"Yeah." Gabrielle summoned a pack of smokes which Furcifer snatched out of her hands.
"You don't want to restart that habit. And most importantly, you want to smoke in my office?"
"Will you stop criticising my coping mechanisms?" Despite her annoyed tone, she made no real attempt to take back the

cigarettes. "It looks like Twitch has the first book."
"That makes all of this a lot harder." Sighed Furcifer.
"Exactly." Gabrielle leaned back in the seat and glanced over him.
Furcifer had hoped that they would be first to find it- making this a race between the IMG and the Elites would give them leverage to bring them to the table. But a third party would make things a lot more complicated.

He nodded slowly and looked back out of the window. It was a lot easier to bury this kind of news when it was literally buried.

As his second in command, Gabrielle could easily come find him whenever she needed him, a privilege she often abused, if only to enjoy the relative quiet of his quarters. He had been put up in the highest flat of the new building, high above the sounds of the street level, in a corner apartment which allowed a lot of natural light into the rooms. Briefly, he wondered if that was why she was here right now. Surely it would have been just as easy for her to call him. But she seemed to be preoccupied with other things, her gaze never straying far from him. Part of him realised that maybe, just maybe, she had come to check he hadn't taken off yet to go after the books alone. As he looked back, he could see she was looking at him expectantly.

"You do know that I don't know his whereabouts right?" Furcifer raised an eyebrow. Twitch and he had been good friends before he had taken this position, but he had burned many bridges in order to get here. Many of his friendships had suffered, perhaps even died, in his quest for knowledge.

"Officially, of course you don't." She narrowed her eyes. "But I know he's been keeping in touch."

"Well that's a big word." He huffed and looked over. "He's been sending clues, yes." He added reluctantly. She already seemed to know anyway. He took out a file from his personal drawer, filled with clippings and postcards.

"And you know him well enough that you could find him if you wanted to." She raised an eyebrow.

Furcifer sighed. "Look, I don't know what you want me to say! I've no real idea where he has been living."

"That you'll find him, Furce." She sighed and sat down. "This is important. You know what the Spell means to him. He's an experienced mage. He could use it and..."

"And what? He wouldn't use it either way." Furcifer interrupted her and turned away from the window.

"Just get to the point, Gabrielle. The other factions have shown interest, to the point that they may buy it from any party who shows interest in selling it. The International Mage Guild is already looking for it and with their global connections, they'll have little trouble finding it in whatever pit of the world Etta and Twitch decided to hide it in." He paced to the window.

"That's why you want this. You're worried they would make money off of a spell written by a member of ours." Furcifer looked over.

She took a deep breath. "You think Twitch might already know where it is?"

"He might or might not." Furcifer was surprised she'd let that sting slide.

"This is no time to speak in riddles, Furcifer." She sat down on his desk.

"It's always time to speak in riddles, Gabrielle."

"You need to stop listening to creepy podcasts. Please promise me this. That you'll find him and check on him. See if he knows about any of this. I mean, The first journal has been found. They're not going to stop."

Furcifer shook his head.

"Alright. Alright." He turned away to sort his thoughts out. This would be hard.

"What about getting the faction leaders identified for the upcoming talks? We still have a lot of work there. Not to mention I've got nine hundred projects to approve of." Furcifer looked over to Gabrielle. "And to sort out our apparent issue with caffeine abuse."

"Oh! You were looking for sympathy? There there." Gabrielle said unconvincingly. "This is your job, last I remembered. Now, are you going out there to find him?"

Ever since joining the Elites, Furcifer had been battling, and Gabrielle knew. At first he'd had to prove himself as a leader when he had never been part of a faction of any kind. Once he had established himself as a decent leader, he'd had to prove himself on every single aspect from filing taxes to writing magic spells. After a few years of this, he had finally managed to become a firm leader, who demanded respect from those who followed him. Gabrielle had given him a lot of support, but he had taught himself well, and fast.

Furcifer looked up again, realising she was still waiting for an answer.

"I do think I know where to find him." He nodded, looking over to the pile of letters he had pulled out. Gabrielle craned her neck as she rifled through them and raised an eyebrow.
"What are those?"
"Letters from random people I believe might be Twitch. Some clippings from newspapers he hid traces of himself in." He put them on his desk and sorted them by date before taking out the most recent one. An assistant digitised everything he collected but he preferred to keep the physical copies of things.
"Now this is a hunch. It might be a random wacko. But this one came from the United Kingdom." He held out a little postcard, not showing her the message on it - it was a personal piece of correspondence after all.

She gave a little shake of her head. "Go on. What are you still doing here?"
"Booking a flight now oh your evil queenness." He snorted.
"I am not amused. And no teleporting now. Until we have a firm law on that, we have to avoid incidents where teleportation plays a role." She walked over to her own office, right next to his. He knew she trusted him, but also that she picked that office for a reason.

The no teleportation rule was a tough one. They were working on laws to ratify all kinds of magic, but this had to be treated separately. Best case, after a year of negotiations or so, it would be ratified like air travel and people would be able to teleport or portal into airports.

Chapter 5

Furcifer breathed in deeply as she left his office. He made sure she was gone, then packed up his correspondence and a few books before leaving for home.

With a sigh he checked his phone for plane tickets. He could teleport there easily and it was very tempting to do so, but it would only make jet lag hit harder once his body realised he had moved through a substantial distance. Ironically mages could go pretty much anywhere magic wise, but the magic cost rose exponentially with the distance. A transatlantic jump cost enough energy to knock out an experienced mage for two days, on top of the jet lag. Governments had been worried about inexperienced mages trying to cross borders and arriving in critical condition. Even with commuter beads, the brunt of the magic fell on the user.

No, it was better to take a flight. He tapped in a few keywords and sighed. At least he didn't have to sort visas out - he had another passport with a currently valid visa under the more regular name of Ronan Johnson. Travelling with a regular name made security checks and other things a lot easier, he'd found. And getting the passport had been easier than expected. People just assumed Atze Furcifer was a fake name, so when he had applied for a British passport he'd been able to fill in the new name. One copy of a fake birth certificate later he had a brand spanking new passport with a different name.

Only indirect flights left. Great. As he gathered the letters one handedly, he booked it and walked to the elevator. At least he was flying Business class.

Home was only a flat in the same building as his office, but it was less accessible to others, which was really the only thing that differentiated it from his office. When the elevator arrived, he put in a key, which took him straight to the penthouse, opening up into the flat he called home. It had a modern interior with a large room doubling as a study and a lounge. Wood walls made the decor look wonderfully elegant, though he honestly did not care. It was mostly a place to lay down his head and sleep, and the only place he could truly be alone these days.

While there was a second toothbrush gathering dust in his bathroom, Gabrielle had her own place. It was rare for her to come over - usually she only spent the night when she had made it too late in her office in the Elite tower. She did not live in the tower, keeping a house quite a few blocks away as her main residence. Furcifer knew there was a reason for it, but she had not confided in him. There were a lot of things they were not telling one another just yet, it seemed.

He sighed and took out a suitcase from under the bed, before grabbing his travel messenger bag. It held his passports, an e-reader, a change of clothes in case the worst happened, a hair brush and a hip flask enchanted to make it unfindable to anyone but him.

What did one pack to go find someone that didn't want to be found, he wondered. Black was always an appropriate colour. He grabbed some black cardigans, a pair of jeans and some shirts. After giving it some thought, he poured a jar of commuter beads into the suitcase as well. He had no idea how long he would be there for but he could always buy more. Money was no longer an obstacle.

Which reminded him, he still needed to put some things in place to find Twitch when he landed. After packing the basics, he started up his laptop and hit up a few people to run an ad in the area he guessed Twitch would be. His fingers hovered over the keyboard as a notification popped up.

There was also something else on his mind - something he had not even told Gabrielle. Alyce Cole, head of the Witches Faction, had approached him about a possible cooperation between Factions. Any other time he would have said no straight away but now things were more difficult.
He sighed and clicked the notification to see what she had replied to his last email. Her first email had been a request to work together in good faith, to which he had responded carefully.
The email was short and to the point, which he always preferred.

"In exchange for a seat at your table we are willing to give up the name of the murderer of Hayden Willemeens."

He slapped the laptop shut with a sharp intake of breath. There had been a rumour the Witch Faction had been responsible for the death of Aiden's wife. Aiden was, or at least had been, a close friend of his before he became the head of the Elite Faction.
But to see the man's pain being used to help a faction?

He opened the laptop up again. Their faction was powerful and they had more people in the United Kingdom, where it seemed this fight would be happening. And if all they wanted was to bring their own knowledge to the table, if anything, this would be a good deal for both of them.

"No deal. I advise you to give that name to the police. If you do I may be willing to include you in the upcoming magic talks." He replied and hit send.

There was no reply. More likely they wanted to give up the name, knowing there would be few consequences. To go to the police and open up the case again would be a whole can of worms they did not seem eager to open up.

Briefly, he wondered if he should let Aiden know. The man had been in jail, accused of his wife's murder. He had almost lost his store, his reputation. But perhaps that chapter was best left closed.

Chapter 6

The sun was just about setting as he made his way to the airport. After paying the taxi driver he made his way in, chuckling on the inside about the fact he was travelling to do research again. It had been a while since he had left the city, which should make this an interesting trip. It was also the first attempt he'd made at actively searching for Twitch ever since the mage had run off. He did not know how the man would respond to him showing up on his doorstep unannounced, but there was no way he could contact him. He would just head to the spot he suspected the man to be and then... see what happened. He rushed through the initial check-in and spied around for his gate, feeling a mixture of annoyance and excitement. England was new territory, it had only a very small, almost non-existent magic scene, and he was excited about the prospect of discovering it.

Security was a breeze - he was usually stopped for his nervous and grumpy manner, but he was smart enough not to pack anything even remotely suspicious. Notebooks and clothes took up most of the stuff in his suitcase. As he opened his bag, he saw a Nosy Nelly crane his neck to look at the contents of his bag.

Strange, he thought, giving the man a glare. After what seemed like an eternity, the customs agent nodded and let him zip the bag up again. He hauled his bag through the rest of the security area then plopped down on a seat near the gate.

He hated flying with a passion. His nails had already been bitten short and he had prepared teleportation spells just in case anything went wrong. A few stray commuter beads were probably knocking around his jacket pocket as well, but he preferred to keep those for emergencies. It wouldn't be the first time they had gotten him out of a tight spot.

At least here he could recharge a bit. People were just relieved to have gotten through security and were mentally preparing for a long flight. Nobody was eager to socialise, and everyone seemed to join him in his moody silence. It was almost perfection - the murmured conversations, people reaching for books and phone chargers. Finally, a moment of solitude in the crowd. He leaned his head back and closed his eyes. Just as he was mentally rehearsing a spell to teleport him to the ground, a figure next to him sat down.

"Great day to fly huh?" The Nosy Nelly from earlier started off, glancing over the mage he had just sat next to.
"There is no such thing." Furcifer grumped, annoyed his bliss had been cut so short. Unfortunately, it did not deter the man's good humour.
"I'm Ramsey Grimes. Treasure hunter." The man looked pale and tall, but with a certain cocky self confidence Furcifer usually liked on a person. Today, not so much. He was not in a socialising mood - not that he ever was.
His phone was pinging constantly with emails from and about faction leaders, looking for information about the upcoming talks. The issue was that there wasn't any information yet - they were still just scouting to make sure there were willing participants for these talks.

"Furcifer. Ground lover." He said, ignoring the outstretched hand. His hands were too sweaty to bother with handshakes.

As he looked around he noticed that boarding was just commencing. As he could imagine nothing worse than tripping over toddlers and squirming past people, the business ticket was worth the money for the early boarding alone. His row would be among one of the first to board.

He was counting on that to get out of this social interaction. He looked intensely at the staff in the boarding area, waiting for his deliverance. In hindsight, maybe he should have walked the extra few metres to the business class airport lounge.

"I know who you are."

Furcifer tensed up, the hairs on the back of his neck standing up. This man was staring at him intently - perhaps he was not just a nosy idiot. He glanced back over to the man, determined not to show that he was intrigued. Or worried.

"Treasure hunter, huh?" A casual question. He'd wished he'd paid more attention to the name now. What was it? Rami something. No. Ramsey and then something with a G.

"Yes. Well, at this point I'm more of a bounty hunter. The

International Mage Guild has set a reward for the person who can find... Oh but I'm sure you already know about it." The man smiled slyly.
"Regale me, treasure hunter." He looked over. He was at a disadvantage in this conversation and it put him in an even worse mood, even though he tried hard not to show it. The man's confidence was now less entertaining and more annoying.

"There is a quite a large reward on finding Asa Ward or any of his notebooks. Only one's been found, so there's six others to be found. And Asa himself of course. It's a lot of money. Think they'll pay per piece or that they only pay out one per hunter?"
Furcifer took a deep breath. This man knew who he was and likely thought he was in contact with Twitch. That's why he was so liberal with information. He expected this contact to pay off.
"Good luck." He said, hoping to end the conversation and relay everything he had learned to Gabrielle right away.
"You're not looking for them?" Ramsey put a hand on his arm as he tried to get up. "It would be a shame, mr Furcifer. You would have such an advantage. There are others looking for it, of course, but you could easily claim the bounty yourself."

"I don't know what you're talking about." He leaned back and reached inside his messenger bag for his magically concealed hip flask, thumb slowly removing the top. As he got up, it tumbled from his bag and spilled its contents onto the man's lap and chest.

"Oh! I'm so sorry!" He exaggeratedly exclaimed. "I'll get you some napkins!" Before he moved, however, he uttered a spell to make the man slur his words. He picked up his bag and rushed to the nearest security guard.

"I'm sorry, sir. I don't mean to be a nuisance but that man over there seems intoxicated. He also grabbed me a few times and warned me not to get on the plane... I wouldn't know why." He said, looking as innocent as he could.

The guard nodded and chattered into his radio for backup just as Furcifer's row was called for boarding. The mage winked at Ramsey as he breezed past the boarding staff and onto the walkway to the plane. The man would not be put off of his quest, but it would make him a bit harder to follow if they weren't on the same plane, especially as it was not a direct flight. And he didn't seem to know he was flying under another name, so hopefully, that would obfuscate the trail even more.

It had almost cheered him up, honestly. Especially as he saw the treasure hunter being pulled away from the gate. He waved and rushed on. If there was one, there were others who were after the Spell. The International Mage Guild was offering money. This meant they were not just interested in reaching mages but humans as well and as some humans made it their profession purely to track people down, that approach could prove very efficient. Money was the universal motivator, and the IMG was good at making it.

Furcifer settled into the plane seat and sighed. As he looked around, he realised that any of these passengers could be a sleuth, looking for Twitch or the journals. To be honest any good detective worth their salt knew it would be easiest to track down a living person rather than a book. People needed food, clothing and social interactions and a lot of that cost money. A trail of money was easy to track down. Credit cards, bank statements, jobs. Tangible things like that gave a person right away.

He had to find Twitch before anyone else did. Whether he wanted their help or not - he had a sneaking suspicion that many of these... treasure hunters would be less kind to him when it came to getting that information.
Gabrielle came to mind.

It had been two years since the events at the university. Back then, many of the newer factions were still forming, relations between the magic communities were being established and Gabrielle had sought out Furcifer to lead the Elites and the Scribes with her. In order to find him, she had set out magical artefacts meant to lure him. When an unwitting museum curator had picked one up and committed a murder under its influence, Gabrielle had offered to undo all she'd done to him, as long as he joined her. Unwilling to join her, he had tried in his own way to clear the man's name. He had lost that battle, but perhaps it had been for the better. He'd had a definite say in how the faction was growing.

Gabrielle is a good leader, he thought as he leaned back in his air plane seat. *But she lacks empathy.*

But most importantly, the one thing Twitch would remember, was the fact that she had tortured him for information.

As the engines fired up, he clutched the armrests. Damnit. The sound coming from all sides was overwhelming, as were the vibrations going through the hull of the plane as they started to taxi and speed up. He shut his eyes tight and hoped for the best. A soft whimper left his lips as the plane left the ground, and he only really opened his eyes once the plane

levelled out. With a deep breath he looked around. Most passengers seemed bored by the tremendous amount of power that had just lifted them off of the ground.
Luckily, it seemed the seat next to him was unoccupied. He briefly flexed his hands and took a deep breath to relax. With a chuckle he wondered if that had been Ramsey's seat.
He called for a stewardess and ordered a double whiskey to make up for the lost booze.

Well. That hadn't been too bad. Now he just needed to stay calm until the landing. Maybe he could work on a long-distance teleportation spell while they were up in the air anyway. He silently repeated the well-prepared teleport-to-ground-safely spell he had kept in mind, just in case. Hands still shaky, he took out a notebook and started making notes.

Chapter 7

Furcifer had opted to take the tube from Heathrow, which in hindsight probably wasn't the best decision. He could not remember the last time he'd seen unfiltered sunlight as he disembarked at King's Cross. It had taken him an hour on a hot train, so as soon as he could he walked out of the station to take in some fresh air. It was not too bad looking a city, he conceded, looking as the streetlights flicked on in the dusk of the day. He stretched his legs with a walk around, tempting himself with but resisting a visit to the British Library. He reminded himself just what was at stake here. He had to keep looking.

Furcifer walked down the stairs of the tube station and breathed in deeply, leaving the large glass building behind. He had put some measures in place to find Twitch, but nothing had worked so far. It had cost him a small fortune but he had bought up advertising space on the tube stations he expected Twitch to at least pass through. He paused in front of one of them and grinned.

He had designed it himself, and he had to admit he had not done a bad job. It looked like a jeweller's ad, if you didn't look too closely, with a fine silver bracelet with braiding pictured on it. It looked very alike the bracelet they had searched for together, only two years earlier. This time he allowed himself a rest and sat down to just people watch for a while. His feet were in pain and he was exhausted, often losing track of the magic he had cast so far. It was a dangerous line to tip toe - if he exhausted himself, he would find himself in trouble in a sprawling and unknown city. After a few minutes, he got up and boarded another train.

Tube stations and signs turned into one big mess of similar looking places, all in shades of burgundy, cream and dark red.
Finally, he ended up at Holborn, sitting down and staring ahead. This place was promising. And if Twitch had taken the bait, he would be here soon. Another one of his ads was staring back at him.

Twitch appeared next to Furcifer. Furcifer sniffed. The magic aura around him did not seem familiar, then again he could have changed it to hide from anyone coming after him.

"Look what the cat dragged in." Twitch said drily. His hair was being blown into his face by the airflow of the passing train, but he didn't even look over to the man next to him. He sounded much more belligerent than Furcifer had remembered him, unlike his meek self. Perhaps he'd had to toughen up on his own.

"Lovely to see you again as well." Furcifer took a deep breath. "We need to talk."
Twitch looked over. "Do we now?"
"Please." Furcifer looked over. "This is important."
Twitch glared a moment then shook his head briefly. "Alright. There's a coffee shop up top."
"I want a donut. Y'guys do donuts?"
"Yes, Furcifer. We do donuts." Twitch sighed and pinched the bridge of his nose. "Come on."

Furcifer was amazed by the sheer amount of coffee shops in this area. Every tube station he had passed through had at least one small stand for coffee. As they entered, he looked around the one Twitch had picked out. He'd been to many a coffee shop, in many different places, but the stiltedness of this place struck him. It was all glass and fake retro wood panelling. He took the ordered coffees and walked towards the table they had occupied, glad to see that Twitch hadn't taken off in the time he had taken to procure the coffee.

"Thanks for the coffee." Twitch took the cup off of his hands.

"Thanks for not running off." Furcifer replied. "How long have you been living here?"

"Just a year."

"Aren't you going to ask how I managed to find you?"

"You put out huge posters on the tube that you were looking for me." Twitch looked unamused. He continued to stir the latte without looking up. "Okay, so it was... subtle for your taste."

"Hey, that cost a lot of money. Even if I only put it up in three stations." He had paid for the ads in three stations, with staggered meeting times in code, so the man had three opportunities to come meet him. It was an ad for a fake jewellery company, with Roman numerals on the bangles spelled out the meeting times and hours.

"Interesting strategy. How's Gabrielle?" Twitch changed the subject quickly.

"Oh. She's good." He nodded. "But... This is not about her."

"Good to hear." He looked over. "That she's fine, at least. I could have guessed you weren't coming here to talk about her."

Furcifer raised an eyebrow as Twitch spoke so calmly about Gabrielle. This was strange. He had half expected the man to not even mention her name.

"It's about the Spell." Furcifer looked over. That had to get his attention.

Twitch's stirring stopped abruptly. "What about it?"'

Furcifer bit his lip and looked down at his hands. His fatigue really bit him now that the exhilaration of finding Twitch was wearing down. A one hour restless nap could not replace a good night's sleep.

"I... Ugh." Furcifer sighed and clenched his hand into a fist. "The International Mage Guild has put a price out to find the Spell. I already had to lose a treasure hunter at the airport."

Twitch sighed. "Fuck."

Furcifer blinked at that sudden interjection. Twitch was not usually someone who cursed, but Furcifer guessed the man had had no idea just how bad it was right now. The rekindled interest in the Spell would make things complicated. The thought of anyone using the Spell for their own interests was horrendous. Surely that was enough to frighten any mage.

But he had never, ever remembered the man swearing like that.

"Yes, fuck." Repeated Furcifer. It was quiet for a while as Furcifer took him in. He looked the same. He sounded the same. Maybe his fatigue was making him paranoid.
"So if I do have the Spell, or know how to find it... What do you want to do with it?" Twitch broke the silence.
"We will put it in the archives to never be used again." He saw the man's face fall. "Or we will destroy it." He added quickly.

"That sounds better." Twitch said. "This is not some silly glitter spell. It's dangerous."
"I know, I know." Furcifer looked over. "I completely understand."
"You don't. Five people died that night. And these were not amateurs but well trained mages." Twitch sipped his coffee and let out a breath as he put it down.

Furcifer shook his head. Now he was sure something was wrong. Twitch would know better than most that four people had died during that ritual, not five. He had better be careful with the information he gave. Just in case. Something about this gave him chills down his spine. The man's tone and voice was off. He'd heard Twitch talk enough in class to know he preferred older terms. Things like "fuck" or "glitter" were not words he used often.

"Look. I don't want anyone to use this. The cost is too high." Twitch looked over to him.
"I completely agree." Furcifer nodded. "That's why I don't want anyone to get this. But they're pulling the stops, Twitch. I've met one treasure hunter. There's probably more of them out there. They put out a monetary reward."
He bit his lip as he looked over the other. He was letting the other side, possibly, know that he knew. Not that anyone had made it a secret. Perhaps it was a good move.

Twitch gulped. "That's huge."
He shivered and drank some more coffee, glancing at something by the counter. Again that strange vibe. Twitch had hated coffee without sugar, but here he was downing it, without milk, leaving the sugar packets on the table untouched.

Furcifer frowned, pretending to search the shoulderbag he had placed next to him, then looked casually behind him.
The man at the counter looked caught and looked away as soon as Furcifer peeked in his direction.
Shit. This was looking a lot more serious. If the fake had brought back up, that meant he was not just here to get some information.

"Well. If you only have the one book, it'll be fine." He got up and looked over. "As long as you keep a hold of that they can't do anything. Bye!"
"You're not leaving are you?" Twitch grabbed the man's arm. Furcifer merely raised an eyebrow.
"Yes I am. I don't think there's anything to worry about." He made a face and looked over with a big smile. He really had to get out - as long as they were in a coffee shop, there was less chance of anything happening. He quickly got to his feet and turned towards the exit.
"Not like they can do the spell with only six books."

"I don't think so." The voice was no longer Twitch's. It was deeper, more... mature. Without turning around he could guess the man had dropped the appearance spell. The jig was up - the steady flow of information had halted.
He looked at the man. The change was almost immediate. The way an experienced mage would have written it. Seeing someone's facial features stretch and contract into another form had made more than one mage lose their lunch. The face in front of him now was a well known one. Salt and pepper hair, almost regal features and wise brown eyes.
"Well." Furcifer wrenched his arm loose as he looked over. "So I finally got your attention, Quentin?"

The leader of the IMG looked over and smiled.

"I guess you did."

Furcifer glanced to the door. The man would not do anything to draw attention inside, but they were only a few paces away from the outside. A steady stream of people trickled through the street, which would force them close together. He sat back down to release the tension on his arm. Furcifer guessed they would make their move soon to force him out of the place.

"So that your spotter there, yeah? He was keeping the magic going?" It was a desperate attempt to keep the man talking and sitting. He had to have something to get him out of this... Until his fingers stumbled across a stray commuter bead in his pocket. Yes! He suddenly felt a lot better about the situation as he met the other's eyes.

Quentin looked over him and raised an eyebrow. "He's with me, yes."

"Getting shaky in your magic in your old age?" It was a common problem for some mages who had been late to magic and who were getting older - their magic became irregular and possibly even unreliable. Quentin was only about fifty-six or fifty seven, but there had been other rumours about his health as well. Furcifer knew the other wouldn't open his heart and tell him all about his struggle, not in this sort of negotiation. But he wanted to know what the other knew about the Spell, why they were so crazy about getting their hands on it.

It worked. Quentin looked over him.
"We're here to discuss this Spell aren't we?" He said.
"We want it for ourselves and we're willing to pay."
Furcifer narrowed his eyes. "For what possible reason? There is no ownership of spells - best we've got is copyright."
"But you're trying to set up the law talks. In a meeting such as that the IMG will discuss ownership of spells. We will push for it. And as the caster's last living descendant is a member of our group..."
"You would be able to claim ownership, but only if you have it." He laughed a little. "I see. But you do know Etta is still alive and she's a member of the Scribes."
"Was a member of the Scribes." Quentin said, before continuing.
"But her work would fall under the Faction's ownership at that time. You're old enough to know how it worked." He winked, though Furcifer did not feel at all joyful.
His hand went to his coat pocket, where he had been stashing the commuter bead. His fingers clenched the familiar item, as if thanking it for being there.

"Well, this was fun... Let's do lunch. I'll have my people call your people." He got up. An arm stretched out to grab him but he was faster, taking a step back and smashing the bead onto the tiles of the coffee shop.

☆☆☆

He grinned as he landed on the floor. That had gone well. He had not slipped them any of their information. But his joy was short lived - the cream carpet and large windows were all too familiar.

“Oh for fuck’s sake.” He groaned as he got up from the floor. He walked to the window of the office. His coffee was already unsettling his stomach after his fast and hard magical escape.

He had teleported himself all the way back to the Elite headquarters in Zeus City. His body had been hurled through miles of magic, crossing back through time zones he had only recently flown through. Pretty soon he would feel even worse as the effects caught up with him. If he was lucky he had just about avoided jetlag. He groaned and reached for his bin, retching into it as his body reacted violently. His air plane lunch, light as it was, was violently expelled before he went completely light headed and fell back onto the rug without wiping his mouth. He held up a hand, but he could see it

double.
"Ooh man..." His stomach reacted again and he reached for the bin again, this time knocking it over. He grabbed for it and hurled into it.
The world's top mage was sprawled on the rug of his fancy penthouse. His nose was bleeding, there was a trail of sick running down his chin and the contents of his paper bin were scattered around him.

Chapter 8

Manon loved when Furcifer left town. It was a great time to go through his book collection, chill in his study, and maybe move some things around when she felt like messing with him. She'd gotten a copy of his key once to help look after the plants in his study, and he'd never asked it back, so why would she have volunteered it? He hadn't even realised he didn't have any plants in his study for her to look after. She hummed and walked around the study, already a heap of books in her arms.

Before working at the IMG, Furcifer had been a professor of magic, and she had been one of his students. He'd gone off to become faction leader, and she had finished her master's before demanding a spot in his faction. She had the talent to back it up.

So now she was working as a researcher for his faction. Still she felt like a child in a candy store when she looked over his collection of books. For all his flaws he had a lovely selection of books and wonders to choose from.

She heard a thunk, followed by a retch, and was immediately on alert. The hair on her arms stood on edge as she put the book down and grabbed a candle stick. There was no way anyone else had snuck in - she was one of the few with a key. She shuffled her feet on the carpet, trying to be as silent as possible. Was some other student taking advantage of the mage's absense? She made her way to the lounge, where she could see a familiar shape lying on the carpet, groaning with effort.

"Furcifer!" She rushed over seeing the man on the ground.
"Manon? What are you doing here?" He carefully turned over to face her.
"That's not important right now. Aren't you supposed to be in London? Did you bring me back marmite?"
"Did I - ugh." He sat up and looked over her. "I fled using a commuter bead and I feel like death and you care only about yeast garbage."
"I hear it's really good on toast." She grabbed a bottle of water from the mini fridge in the study and opened it for

him.

"Drink some." She encouraged.

"Nothing stronger?"

"Keep that in and I'll see what we can do." She said, raising an eyebrow at him. Long magic commutes like the one he had just done took a toll on a body.

He groaned but sipped from the bottle. "What's going on? What are you doing in my flat?"

She shrugged. "I just came to raid your library." She looked over and bit her lip. "You guys are after that secret project right? I've heard there's something similar going on in the IMG."

"How -" He frowned. The IMG were secretive. They didn't exactly publish a blog about the stuff they were up to.

"I'm kind of dating a girl who is in their programme?" She grimaced. "Her name's Rebecca."

Furcifer laughed. "So what's she been telling you?"

She looked at him thoughtfully. "Just that there's been talk about a secret project. Something big that goes straight to the top. And they're going to make a public announcement in..." She checked her watch. "About two hours."

"Alright. Let's order in some coffee. I want to be awake for that."

Manon grinned. "Gladly." There was an expensive artisanal coffee shop next to the building, some interns eager to please and she had his credit card. This would be fun.

Chapter 9

Twitch quickly ducked away from the coffee shop Furcifer had vanished from. It had only been seconds since he had seen Furcifer jump up and smash the bead on the floor, vanishing into thin air. Crude, but effective. The two men walked outside, but it was clear they knew they had lost him. After a peek around, they walked away from the shop.

Twitch had seen the ads in the tube recently, but he had been unsure whether to actually go and see the man. In the end he had decided to go meet him, but he had seen Furcifer with the imposter just in time to hide.

It was an eery feeling to see an exact copy of yourself talking to someone you knew. It had taken everything he had not to step in and burst out at the man pretending to be him. At least now he could guess that Furcifer was here for the notebooks. Nobody would go through such great lengths to impersonate him just to have a chat with Furcifer. In fact, it was something most people tended to avoid.

He sighed and put his hood up as he walked away from the coffee shop. The little melting shards of the commuter bead sparkling on the floor told him Furcifer had teleported out of there. Due to the mass of people streaming in and out of the office buildings nearby he'd not had a clear view of the two people chatting as soon as they had gone into the coffee shop.

Why did he have to get his stupid self involved? Twitch shook his head. Furcifer and him had parted on okay terms, definitely not good enough terms for the other to offer his help out of the sheer kindness of his heart. Now that he knew the Spell was in play, he probably wanted to get his hands on it.

Well, if he thought Twitch was just going to gush over the leader of some fancy faction and run to him for help... He was just about right.

Twitch had never been a grandiose man, and he knew he was out of his depth here. Any ally doing it for the right reasons was a good one. He peeked behind him, and noticing he was not being followed, made his way home. As he walked, he checked his phone to see if he still had Furcifer's number, and dialled it.

"Hello?" Gabrielle answered the phone.
It was only one word, but it felt like a gut punch. He almost dropped the phone and had to fumble to hang up. Immediately his palms clammed up and he had trouble hanging on to the plastic rectangle in his hands. His stomach fell. It was very likely that help from Furcifer came with Gabrielle in tow, and he could not face her, not yet.

The two of them were close, perhaps even lovers by now. Just the thought of her with his friend.... He shivered and walked back home. Perhaps he could do this on his own.

Chapter 10

"It's starting soon." Manon rushed up to get into the couch. With some magic and a lot of effort, Furcifer had made it to the sofa. He definitely regretted it now - the extra magic weighed on him like a brick. He was exhausted and he'd need at least two days of sleep to recover from his magic trip.

Gabrielle made a face at his phone and shrugged before walking over.

"You got a call from a... Sandy?" She blinked. "Hung up when I answered."

Sandy. That rang a bell but Furcifer couldn't place it right now.

"I'll look at it later. It's probably the pitch for the anti caffeine project." He sighed and looked over.

Gabrielle glanced over. "Alright. What are you guys watching?"

The tv was tuned to one of the local channels dedicated to magic news. It usually only aired a few reruns of their homebrew shows about magic and magic awareness, more like a human interest channel than anything else. Today, however, a reporter was standing in a meeting room in a large building, which Furcifer briefly recognised as belonging to the IMG. Their headquarters in London, if he was not mistaken. Their largest headquarters were in Brussels, but it was unlikely any press would show up there. It was a good decision for them to use their building in the United Kingdom. He sat up a bit straighter, wincing at the pain in his back. Currently, the reporter was describing the building of the IMG as if she was describing a fairy tale castle. By now Furcifer knew that the windows had gorgeous velvet curtains, chosen for their luscious sheen, but nothing about the improvised little press conference they were doing.

"We are just seeing Quentin arrive in the meeting room." The reporter continued, and the camera shifted to see the man arrive at the front of the room. On the table in front of him there was a laptop, and a large tv was set up behind him.
"This should be good." Gabrielle dropped the phone on Furcifer's lap, making him wince.

Quentin looked at the camera.
"My name is Quentin and I am the leader of the International Mage Guild. Currently we are the largest faction in terms of people, and we are active globally." He paced around as the screen behind him started up.

"As its leader I have spent the last five years helping this faction get to the very top, reaching out and helping people to find their true power. We have always extended our hand to anyone who would join us and beaten any challenge that has arisen."

"As such, we were among the first to accept when the leader of the Elites, Atze Furcifer, reached out to us to join his round table discussion around the laws of magic."

"You lying -" Furcifer hissed.

Manon shushed him, holding a finger up.

"... important as that discussion may be, we have decided to not participate in it. We have strong evidence to suggest Furcifer was responsible for the theft of one of our spell tomes. Furthermore, he and his accomplice are guilty of torturing and imprisoning a mage falsely. This is not the kind of person we wish to talk to when it comes to peace among ourselves and others."

"From the start he has not been forthcoming with information, while we as an organisation cherish the freedom of knowledge. As such we have turned over the evidence we have to the police. Lastly, Twitch... If you're out there, we are willing to help you. Come find us in any of our offices whenever. That's all I have for now. Thank you for joining us today, Carine. And to you at home, thank you." He walked off, leaving the reporter mute.

The screen behind Quentin was now playing an audio track

that had come from the headquarters of the Scribes.
Twitch begging for mercy and the sound of a raging fire.
"How the fuck did they get this!" Gabrielle got up with a gasp. "Fuck. Fuck!"
"That's what you're worried about?" Manon looked over. "It's worse for the talks than anything else, right?" But even she seemed nervous.
"There might be a warrant out on us for this." Gabrielle said softly.
"Getting us arrested would keep us from going back to the UK. And we've just lost any goodwill among mages." Furcifer closed his eyes, wishing the painkiller would kick in.
The talks would be over before they even started. Worst of all - a part of it was true. Gabrielle had tortured Twitch so it would not be a stretch to assume all of it was true.

"Turn that off!" The sounds continued.
Gabrielle hid her face in her hands.

Chapter 11

Ethan looked up from his desk as the head of the IMG stepped in. It was usually quite a great honour, but the last few days he had seen more of the man than he cared for.
He got up from his seat, more out of habit than actual respect.
"Good afternoon, sir. How did the press conference go?" He asked, hoping to get a positive answer. It would at least put the man in a better mood. He was surprised to see him so soon, as he had probably only just gotten off of the Eurostar into Brussels.

"I think it will be sufficient." The man nodded. "I have him on the ropes, Ethan. It's wonderful."
Ethan shivered a bit. They had just accused the head of a rival faction of stealing from them and torturing a fellow mage. There would be a backlash.

"How are you doing with the notebook?"
One notebook had been found by them legitimately. Purchased from a private collector, it had been verified as one of the notebooks in which Etta had hid her spells. The second book they had had vanished, leading Quentin to believe it had been stolen by Furcifer.
Little did he know that Ethan himself had taken it to hide it away from this power hungry group.

He smiled a little at the leader. "You'll be pleased to hear I've made some progress. The notebook appears to be a mystery, but it's quite simple. Most spells in here are actually not spells at all." He grinned. That brought him some pleasure - the thought of his mother just thinking up random coconut milking spells to fill up empty pages.
"Some seem to be generated from random phrases, but others are just... silly spells, unless you want a spell that empties your gas tank." He chuckled.

"Wonderful." Said Quentin, walking over. Ethan closed the book he was reading and put it away.
Quentin raised an eyebrow but didn't ask.
"We would like for you to attend an event in the United Kingdom, Ethan."
Ethan raised an eyebrow. He was a researcher, little more. It was rare for him to be sent to events... Unless the other didn't

want him here.
Vaguely, he realised the other was waiting for an answer.
"I understand." He simply said.
"It's merely us showing our goodwill." Quentin waved a hand. "Dean Mara Terry was one of the first to introduce magic classes at her university and she's doing a fundraiser for a similar cause in the UK now that she's moved back. She's heading up an organisation to help teachers learn how to work with magic children. We'd like for you to represent us there."
"I would be more than happy to." Ethan said, without much joy. Despite his researcher status, he was quite highly ranked. Usually there would be talk about him becoming one of the leaders, but that would not happen.

Ethan was growing old. Next year he would be fifty, and his hair was greying much like Quentin's. Much like Quentin, he was still quite fit and ate well. Unlike many mages, he did not let his studies engulf him so much that he did not make time for exercise and cooking his own meals rather than grow dependant on the Guild's cookery. Many of the ones who had joined the guild had also moved here from outside of Belgium, making them even more dependent on the Guild.

"So, when will you find the next spell book?" Quentin asked after a pause.

Ethan immediately turned his nose up, a knee-jerk reaction.

"Sir, we've only just found this book. We need to study it to find clues as to where the next one is." He said simply. "We'll need time."

"How much time?" Quentin's tone was suddenly a lot less amicable.

"At least a few days, if not a week. Sir, we're still analysing this book and it's the first of its kind we've had a chance to study! I-"

"I don't want to hear it, Ethan. I expect there might be more of those books hidden in the UK, after all, that's where we found the first. We've got blessed little time to find these things. Don't disappoint me." The head of the Guild turned his back on the man and made his way out.

Ethan let out a breath. This was going to be complicated. He knew the man's plan - somewhat. There was a lot of mystery shrouding the higher echelons of the party these days. Only selected mages had been invited into the meeting before this press conference. The last few years, the Guild had changed considerably. The Guild had flourished under the former head of the Guild, a charismatic leader named Redford, until his death. In difficult times Quentin had turned to the past. It seemed he was planning to do the same thing now.

Ethan had been averse to the plan from day one, feeling they should embrace the future not the past. If it wasn't for Quentin's own damn self loathing... Nevertheless he had joined the efforts due to his link to the Spell, and hopefully to prove to the man that the Spell was not the way.

Nevertheless he had joined the efforts due to his link to the Spell, and hopefully to prove to the man that the Spell was not the way. Quentin, on the other hand, would not budge and had even suggested Ethan should be part of the mages to perform the spell.

Well. Not if he could help it. He had already spoken to a group of mages, most of whom had left after voicing their concern about the Spell and not being taken seriously. Some had merely joined Ethan's group after hearing about the search for the Spell. They were laying low either in other factions or on their own, with one thing in common.

None of them wanted to see the Spell used.

Chapter 12

Furcifer had given himself three days to recover from the sudden transatlantic jump. He still felt somewhat nauseous thinking about any kind of portal magic, but he was doing a lot better.

He had contacted Twitch on his own, glad the man even wanted to talk to him. It had taken some convincing.

But none of that was the reason that Furcifer still looked like death.

They had soon discovered that the only way to get back to the United Kingdom was to portal back.

Furcifer retched as soon as he arrived in the courtyard and threw up in a bush before straightening up. At least he had landed closer to Twitch this time, which was his only consolation. Jet lag would hit soon and he still had a lot to do.

The building Twitch was living in was an old converted mansion, made into flats. There were six main entrances looking out over a courtyard, the flat numbers painted above the doorways. With some cursing, Furcifer found the correct doorbell.

"It's me." He grumped, before being let in through the communal door. He immediately saw the short mage, standing in the doorway, lit by the light streaming from his flat.

"Why is your name not on that doorbell?"

"It is. My name is Asa Ward." Twitch opened the door wider to let him in.

"You're grumpy."

"I just spent two days in bed, recovering from a transatlantic commuting bead, then I had to take another long haul flight here! Not to mention how I'll be able to get back." His entrance with the Ronan Johnson passport had been logged, so he'd had to use his other one. It would take a lot of fighting with the embassy to get that sorted, if they even could get it sorted. Explaining why he had entered the country on two different passports would be hard, and he doubted they would accept "I was in a hurry" as an excuse. And if there was an arrest warrant out on Atze Furcifer, he wouldn't even make it out of the country. Gabrielle had come with, but there was no indication she would be any safer. He jumped a little as he felt something brush by his leg.

"Mind the cat. Gothball is not allowed outside." Said Twitch, opening the door to his flat.

Tiny, but workable. He could see the lounge and kitchen at first glance, with a small row of herbs growing on the window sill.

"You... have a cat. A black cat." Furcifer sighed, his gaze drawn to the tuxedo cat jumping onto the sofa.

Twitch chuckled. "I adopted it ages ago. Cats are good at smelling out bad magic."

"Should take it out on a leash." Furcifer replied dryly, plopping himself just next to the cat.

Twitch ran a hand through his hair and looked over to the man.

"How has Aiden been?" Twitch asked, and Furcifer could tell he needed some space before they talked about the spell.

"He's been... good. Jeffrey is helping him run the store, he's teaching part time at the university and all that..." He

shrugged.
"I miss the store." Twitch admitted.
"It's a good store." Furcifer didn't go deeper into that end of the conversation. He was not here to talk
"You saw the press conference the IMG did?"
"Unfortunately." Twitch said. "I've not been able to sleep since –"
Furcifer merely nodded. He couldn't imagine what the man had gone through but he was suddenly happy he had asked Gabrielle to stay behind.
"Be honest. Is Gabrielle here?" Twitch looked over.
"She's in London." He had to admit. "There's an apartment the Faction owns...." He shrugged. He didn't want to say too much about it.

Twitch shrugged and sat down on the other side of the cat, who just stretched out and climbed onto his lap.
A brief silence floated between them as he petted the cat on his lap.

"I want you to know something." Twitch started.
"Don't give me this." Furcifer's head lulled back. "We know this Spell is dangerous." And his head was killing him right now. "Hey, do you have any aspirin?"
"I can give you some ibuprofen." Twitch got up and walked to the medicine cupboard in his bathroom before handing two

tablets to the redhead, along with a glass of water.
"Thanks... And rest assured- "
"Yes but... I did not ask for any of this." Twitch looked over. "It was meant for another witch, not me. Plenty of people think I'm not worthy."
Furcifer lifted his head, his interest piqued. "You think they might be after you?"
"I'm not saying that. But I don't have a untouchable status either. If the IMG grabs me, they might... interrogate me." He shivered. Gothball was not impressed, and sought out the area between the two men again.

"And they won't care if you live or well, die." Furcifer finished his train of thought.
"Exactly." Gothball jumped up as Twitch got up and walked to a cupboard.
"I've copied every page in this notebook, and the letter Etta gave me. It's the one she sent Redford after hiding the books. Before all of this they had apparently been good friends, and she was really into the idea of an international faction... She thought it was the only way a faction could work. He sent the letter back, apparently he was disgusted by her actions and severed all ties. But it contains the locations of the other books. Not exactly well written out clues but drawings, riddles... it should also contain the first part of the Spell."
Furcifer got up. "You're just... giving this to me?"

"I have no choice. We'll have to split up to find every book in time." Twitch handed over a thick manilla envelope. "I've not figured out which spell in this book is part of the Spell. I suspect we'd need all seven books to do that."

"That would make sense." Furcifer nodded, resisting the urge to rifle through the envelope right there and now. "Thank you. I mean it. We will finish what they started."

Twitch sighed. "No. We will put it to rest."

Chapter 13

He was getting too old to sleep on people's sofas, Furcifer realised. Part of his leg was sticking to the fake leather seat of Twitch's sofa, his arm was numb from lying on a bumpy part, and he had woken up once or twice to find Gothball snoring on his chest. In the end he guessed he'd gotten about six straight hours of sleep. Good enough, usually. Not enough to get him to the top of his game, but even below the top of his game he was better than most. It had been a lot easier to crash on the couch than to take the tube back to the hotel close to midnight, when they had stopped talking.

He unplugged his phone from the charger and groaned. A heap of notifications.
The results of his physical, demanded by Gabrielle after the large jump, had come. An email informed him he was mildly anemic and to grab some iron tablets from the nearest pharmacy. The news that the IMG was not attending the law conference talks had made waves - other factions were thinking of following suit. As one of the larger factions, the IMG had a lot of pull.

There was no news about whether or not he and Gabrielle would be wanted for questioning. But the police would not make that public knowledge until they had been arrested. There were only a few options. They could turn themselves in and hope for the best, try and explain why their first reaction was to take a plane out, or wait to be arrested. For now they had been in touch with their lawyers, and the expensive legal team was on standby if they were arrested while out of the country.

Twitch brought over a cup of tea and a plate with some toast.

"Morning, sleepy head. We need to get going soon."

"Go where?" Furcifer glanced at his phone. Many missed calls and texts from different groups. Aiden had even texted him. Things had to be bad for Aiden to get worried about him. Or maybe he was just texting him to go burn in hell. Either way. He put the phone down with a yawn. Briefly, he thought back about the email, where a Witch Coven member had offered him the name of Hayden Willemeens' murderer. He hadn't even given the question whether to tell him another thought.

"I've found the second book. It's with a wise man named Salem." He said. "We'll have to pick it up."

Furcifer sipped the tea, then drank it in one go. "Can I get another one of those?"

Chapter 14

Twitch walked silently for a bit. This time, he could see the Elites spokesperson on the electronics store TVs they passed. He hadn't told Furcifer, but apparently Gabrielle and he were now wanted for questioning. He was sure they knew, either way. They had fancy lawyers and all that. Still, if they weren't careful, the other mage's help would be short lived.

Furcifer grinned. Some tea and a shower had helped him immensely, it seemed. He folded open a paper map and glanced over it.

"So where is the next journal? Museum of London? Oh! Bart's Pathology museum!"

"Nope." Twitch turned towards a little stand with a flashing sign in red, yellow and purple.

"Where else would a magical wise man - oh, you picking up some burner phones?" Furcifer asked as Twitch approached a phone stand with malfunctioning neon lettering.

MOBILE PHONE UNLOCKING

SCREEN REPAIR

TELEPHONE CARDS

Furcifer sighed. “You’re kidding me. It’s at a... stand.” Disenchanted, he folded up his paper map.

“Yep.” Twitch said. The little stand was half embedded between two buildings, providing just enough space for the person manning it to turn around. The front consisted of a small glass cupboard, with feature phones, cheap smart phones and even a few old fashioned flip phones. The lower shelves mostly had cables, telephone cards and adapters.

Furcifer took a deep breath and looked over to Twitch. Great. A mage - just after he and his Faction had been accused of stealing spells and torturing a mage. He just hoped the man would not be belligerent.

In a way it was a masterstroke of the IMG not to release a picture of Twitch. Twitch would get sympathy and help, if they knew what he looked like. Without that information, he just seemed to be one of Furcifer's helpers.

“Go on then.” Furcifer kept his distance a little. His photo hadn't been on the tv, but it was easy enough to look up what he looked like.

Twitch nodded and turned to the man behind the stand. "Etta sent me to collect her property."

"Doesn't ring a bell." The man didn't look up from the farm game on his tablet. The man had dark, deep eyes which seemed to sparkle a bit when he saw him. Strange.

Twitch sighed and thought. Of course he wouldn't be jumping and eager to hand over the item. He would have to prove he had magic himself. Peering into the booth he saw a lot of random plugs and extension cords. A show of water magic might not be a good idea. Wind? Could easily be explained away.

In the end he closed his hand and opened it again, showing a small black lump of coal. He closed his hand again and squeezed, turning it into a small diamond.

"Do you remember her now?" He asked. "Or Ethan. He might have dropped it off on the way here."

"Now that you mention it." The man raised an eyebrow. "But how do I know you're the one I'm meant to give it to?"

Twitch looked around for a second then dove into his bag, taking out the first notebook.

"This should suffice."

Salem grabbed the book and paged through it.
"It's actually real!" He laughed, before handing it back.
"One moment." He held up a finger and turned behind him, finding a tablet computer and unplugging it from the charger. It was about seven inches, black front and back. Nothing special about it.
"There is of course a storage fee. I've had to digitise the book I received as it was very badly damaged..."

Twitch's mind wandered as he watched the man's studied movements, his careful manner. There was something in the way he moved and despite the fact that he was running a phone stand, he did not seem very confident in handling the tablet. He was ancient, but in a young body. Rich brown eyes which had seen a lot of pain and misery. He seemed familiar, but he couldn't place it.
"You're one of the immortals!" Furcifer gasped, and Twitch lost his train of thought. Twitch blinked - there were only a few confirmed immortals. Generally they were longer lived individuals. The few confirmed ones there were had lifespans of up to 300 years. As there were only about five of them, their photos were well known throughout the magic community. Twitch had never really studied them, but he guessed it was part of Furcifer's job to know.

"No shit, Sherlock. Who's the yankee?"
"A friend." Twitch said. "So! We were discussing a fee?" Steering the conversation back to the money was likely to diffuse the situation.
"Who still says yankee?" Furcifer raised an eyebrow.
"I do, you nincompoop. Now please be quiet while the adults talk. It'll be five hundred... "
Twitch wished his phone had a camera. Furcifer's insulted face made his day.
"What are you going to do, turn some lead into gold?" Furcifer crossed his arms.
"Sure. Have you figured that one out yet?" He took an old fashioned coil of tin-lead soldering wire.
"I bet you a hundred of your monopoly money you can't turn it into gold."
"Two hundred." Said Salem, smirking.
"This I've got to see. Alright. Two hundred, but no back up."
Salem grinned and uttered a spell, before taking something out of a flask and pouring a few drops onto the metal. Within seconds the wire crackled, and spots of gold appeared in the wire.
"You're... Kidding me!" Furcifer grinned and picked up the coil to examine it. "You win this one, old timer." Furcifer reluctantly counted out two hundred pounds and handed it over.

"So. We were discussing a price for the tablet..." Twitch tried weakly. He really didn't want to spend much more time here - if left to his own devices Furcifer would start a tiny magic war with this man.
"Three hundred." Salem nodded and sat back down. "Your friend managed to get you a discount. But payable now before you take it away."
"Of course." Twitch dug around in his pockets, even though he knew he did not have that much cash on him. Reluctantly he held out his credit card.
"There. Charge it."
"Beautiful!" The man's eyes lit up as he processed the transaction, handing over the tablet and credit card in one movement.
"My name is Salem, it has been a pleasure."
"Not Methusalem?" Snickered Furcifer, earning him a glare.
"Please ignore him. He's... Not from around here." Smiled Twitch.
"It's been a pleasure, Salem." He put the card and tablet away in his messenger bag and turned. Best not to leave any names. If they were after him, too much information would not do anyone any good.

"Alright. That was fun." Furcifer walked away with him. "Can you believe that guy? He just... gold!" He looked flabbergasted still, which at least took some of the edge of the high cost off.
"For you. Three hundred is a lot of money you know." Groaned Twitch.
"I'll pay you back." He waved his hand and looked over.
"Good. Make yourself useful."
Furcifer snorted. "I like your new attitude. Usually a bad sign."
Twitch blinked and stopped abruptly as a car skidded to a halt near the stand. Inside of the car, he could see them debating and looking around. It looked like they were following something on

"Not local." Twitch simply said before doing a U-turn.
"So?" Furcifer wondered before he caught on. "Shit."
As two men exited the car he turned with Twitch and started walking away.

"How did they find us? I only used localised magic!" Twitch hissed as he sped up the pace. Localised magic, like small spells, could only be sensed by other mages within a three meter radius. There was no way anyone had sensed that magic unless they had passed by exactly during the five seconds it had taken him to perform the magic.
"Let's go." Furcifer said, walking ahead of him. "These guys are good. Oooh yes, they must have some-"

Twitch didn't listen, glancing over to the car as they weaved through the busy mass of people on the kerb.
He knew he was clear - they didn't seem to focus on him. They were looking at Furcifer. It would make sense that they had some sort of tracker on him. The two who had gotten out of the car were catching up.

"Can you stop praising them long enough to run!" Twitch started running towards a bus stop.
Furcifer nodded and Twitch just hoped he was following. Buses would be a pain to follow on foot and the men already had a hard time navigating the crowd on the pavement. As long as they got to a bus in time, they would be fine. He glanced back, but the men barely stood out in the crowd.

Twitch nimbly jumped on board of a waiting bus, shoving his oyster card on the reader before moving to the top deck of the bus. He rushed to a seat and checked over his messenger bag, running his hand over it and taking a deep breath. He'd made it. The tablet was still there as well. With a bit of a jerk, the bus took off into traffic.

Crap. Where was Furcifer? He'd hopefully made it onto another bus. He would be smart enough to know not to come to his house straight away just in case they were being followed. Somehow he doubted the men would be able to follow this far - they had come by car to the busy centre of the city. They did not seem like the type to know the bus routes and pedestrian walkways which he had used so many times. They were not local.

But neither was Furcifer. He leaned his head back then grabbed his phone.

`Please tell me you made it. Meet me at coffee shop near the funny station name.`

There was a busy coffee shop just close to Cockfosters, a name Furcifer had found hilarious when first seeing it on a map. It also had decent wi-fi so he would be able to upload the notebook to his personal cloud storage.

Etta had warned him not to expect all notebooks to be the same, but this was absurd. It would take ages to either digitise the other books or to print off the entirety of this digital copy. It was smart though. Making all the books look alike would make things a little too easy.

He opened up the one file the tablet held. It was aptly named "Spells.pdf". Scanning through it, he could already tell that it was a lot larger than most of the other spellbooks and it was still loading up the file. His eyes landed on one page.

Chapter 15

Furcifer had completely lost track of Twitch. He had seen the man run towards a bus, but the doors had closed in front of him. Unwilling to stand around and wait he had run for the next stop and hopped onto the back of a bus with an open back door, riding it a few stops before getting off.

It seemed he was easier to follow than Twitch. He needed to think fast. He was being followed. Two of them he had noticed - one in a patterned shirt and the other, Ramsey. Had the man put a tracker on him when they met at the airport? It was very likely. He tried to think which items he had on him right now which he'd had with him on the plane. Planting the tracker after security was smart, he had to admit. It had probably been slipped into a jacket pocket or something, or in his messenger bag.

He calmed down. Now that he knew how they'd found him, he could work against them. Also, it made him realise they had no idea what Twitch looked like, so it was rather lucky they had split up. He kept walking, head down, digging into his bag.

Suddenly he felt a hand on his butt, and he raised an eyebrow. He focused back on his surroundings.

A familiar stench was forming next to him, and he glanced to his left.
"Ramsey. What a pleasant surprise." He sighed. Just what he needed.
"Fancy seeing you here!" Blinked the man, faking surprise.
"Was that you I felt rummaging through my back pocket?" Despite the situation, he almost made it sound flirty.
Ramsey raised an eyebrow. "That wasn't me. That might have been an actual pickpocket." He said, keeping pace with the man as they walked.
"Motherf-" Furcifer quickly searched for his wallet, relieved to find it in his front pocket still.
"I heard you found the second notebook. Well done." He smiled a little.
"News travels fast. Did you bug me?" He wondered, looking up to the man.

"Wouldn't you like to know." He winked. "We've already found one of the notebooks."
"Really now? I don't believe you." He stopped and looked over.
"Keep walking. Londoners don't like to be stopped in their tracks." Said Ramsey, glancing around and keeping up the pace.
"You are in trouble, Furcifer. There is no way you can find all the books in time."
"I'm not alone. Now that was you touching my butt now wasn't it?" He raised an eyebrow.
"Oh, yes it - " Ramsey was cut off by a punch in the face. Furcifer didn't see who it was at first - just a whirlwind of silver hair.

Gabrielle took Furcifer's hand and dragged him down an alley.
"You boys screwing things up again?" She sighed as she cast a spell and pushed the both of them up against the wall. "Invisibility. They'll walk right past us."
"Or into us. Ow!" Furcifer huffed as he was bumped into by a confused commuter taking a shortcut. He was starting to feel the tingle of the spell on his exposed skin, or it maybe it was just her touch.
"I made us invisible, not intangible." She pressed her back against the wall. "And not inaudible either."

"Twitch didn't want you here." He hissed.
"I know, but you're making a mess of things." Gabrielle whispered back.
Furcifer quieted down as Ramsey regained his balance and glanced around to try and find him. The two of them stayed quiet until Ramsey walked off, trying to find his co-conspirator, no doubt."
"You didn't trust me?"
"There's been a development. The Guild found one of the journals."
"Shit. Ramsey was telling the truth."
"Yes, shit. If they have one, it's not a big deal. Neither of us would be able to use the Spell. But if they find a second or third one..."
"They might have enough to start reverse engineering it. I think he's gone."
"Few more minutes."
"Are you enjoying this, Gabrielle?" He looked over with a smirk.
Gabrielle rubbed her temples. "You're an occupational hazard more than anything. Now we should be good." She shifted off

the invisibility slowly.
"Twitch is waiting for me." He said, reading the text on his phone. "I'm guessing you'll want to come to break the bad news."
"Oh thanks." She scrunched her nose and looked over. "So any luck on the hunt so far?"
"Twitch now has two of the books. Four out there still."
"That's something I guess." She sighed. "Lead the way."

Furcifer quickly checked his paper map. "This is Finsbury park. We need to get underground and get the Piccadilly line." He nodded and looked for an entrance. "There!"
He walked with her to the tube station. "So you came all this way just to tell me about the found notebook?"
"I don't know who to trust, Furcifer. How did they get that audio?"
He knew exactly what she was talking about. There was no way she would have recorded herself torturing another mage. Had they had a bug in her old office? If so what else did they know?

As they entered the windy corridor for the tube, her hair was flicked in front of her face, and placed back behind her ear with a swift hand.
"It's not unlikely they have a mole either. Manon has a person on the inside with the Guild." He sighed. "This is our train."

He nodded as the train stopped in front of them.
“If we get separated, get off at Cockfosters and find the green coffeeshop. It should be the final stop.”
She nodded briefly. “Gotcha. Also wanted to make sure you’re safe. And seems like I was right to be careful.”
“Maybe.” Furcifer shrugged. “But I was doing just fine.”
“Riiight.” She looked over. “So you were flirting with that treasure hunter?”
“Why, would you be jealous?” He smirked, already knowing the answer.

Chapter 16

The coffee shop was half empty as the two of them entered - perhaps not a popular time to get coffee. Furcifer looked around for Twitch, and saw his head shoot up when he saw the two of them. Even worse, Twitch immediately picked up his bag when he spotted Gabrielle.

"Twitch." Furcifer moved over quickly. "Look. She helped me lose Ramsey." He added quickly, hoping that would help. If she was useful to them, there was no way he could tell her to leave right?

"Who?" Frowned Twitch. "Either way, I don't care. I don't want her here." He shook his head and glanced over to her.

With a shiver, Furcifer could see the hairs on the back of

Twitch's neck stand up.
"Let's just be civil about this?" Furcifer asked.
"Civil?" Guffawed Twitch. "I told you my terms! I don't want her here yet you bring her here and you expect me to just... shrug it off and go about my day? Well I will be going about my day, you just won't be there."
"Look, she can be valuable." Furcifer said, but immediately he could see that had been the wrong thing to say.

"That is not what we agreed upon. You were going to come here without her. If you can't help me without her... Then I guess you can't help me." He made a face at Gabrielle and walked off towards the door. By now he had slung his backpack onto his shoulders and was ready to leave.

Furcifer sighed. It looked like the broadcast had opened up old wounds, and he couldn't blame Twitch. But it still hurt.
"Don't come to my house. Not with her." Twitch turned around once more before shaking his head and walking out.

Furcifer sagged onto a seat and saw the man speed off. He did not even glance over to them.
"That went well." Furcifer shook his head.
"I know, I had expected that." Gabrielle looked over the list of coffees. "You... you saw the show the IMG put up. He's had those wounds torn open."
Furcifer looked over. She really did understand feelings - sometimes he wondered what was really under that hard shell. Sometimes he could spot a very caring, compassionate person. But most of the time the acerbic wit between them was all he needed.

"I guess." Furcifer relented and peeked at the menu. "What do you want?"
"World peace, that notebook and an americano."
"Can do you an amaretti cookie, a coffee and... a note pad?"
"I'll take the cookie and the coffee. Thanks." She said and looked over. "So did you figure out how they found you earlier?"
Furcifer nodded and took a napkin, writing on it that he guessed it was in his bag somehow, and pushed it over to her. She nodded and grabbed his bag. She combed through the contents but then handed it back with a shrug.
She shook her head and then took the napkin, writing Aiden's name on it.

"No, I haven't figured out how they found me." Furcifer replied carelessly. "Guess we'll find out."

Damn, if she couldn't sense the tracker there were only a few options. He could ditch the bag and only take his essentials, but that didn't mean he didn't accidentally grab the tracker.

Gabrielle's suggestion was the best - Aiden was an electric mage who could find these kinds of things. He would have to contact him tonight. Briefly he checked the message the man had sent him that morning - just a general "Saw the news, you okay?" text, but it was still sweet.

He sent back a quick text.

`Yes, thanks. May need your help later. Please give my love to Oni and whatsisname`

He put the phone away and got up to go order.

After coffee, they'd taken a long walk to make sure there was nobody following them. There was no specific place to go, they just wandered through the parks and looked through a few shops. The mood between them was tense. Gabrielle didn't say it, but she had been taken aback by Twitch's refusal to work with her. She understood, he knew. Otherwise she would have argued. Their conversations slowly grew slower and ended. When he could see Gabrielle was growing tired of the walking around, he'd steered them back to their flat. The signals were always clear to him - she'd stop being chatty and just cross her arms as if cold.

Seconds after getting into the room, he started stripping.
Gabrielle raised an eyebrow, though her eyes did travel over him.
He rolled his eyes right back at her and tried to mime out a bug. The look on her face was priceless.
"I'm just thinking I should change, is all." He nodded over to the bag. If he changed outfit into something completely from his suitcase, new shoes and all, and left his bag in the hotel, it was unlikely he would be tracked.
"Don't bother on my account. No plans." She seemed to have caught on.
He opened up the suitcase and rummaged through it for an outfit. Leaving his messenger bag with phone and ID behind

would be cumbersome, but the last thing he wanted was for them to be followed straight to Twitch's place.

Gabrielle nodded over to his shoes, raising an eyebrow. She knew him too well - he'd only brought one pair, but he was reasonably certain those had been safe. He sat down with a frown and started rummaging through them, holding them upside down.

"Oh, no plans?" He said airily, keeping the conversation going. When every word was overheard, it seemed hard to be genuine, so he just flirted.

"I don't know, you want to plan something with me?" She giggled flirtily.

Furcifer noticed his mouth was open and he closed it quickly. "Ah, uh."

"Cause I have a budget spreadsheet you haven't even looked at and it is due Monday." She added, tone drastically changed.

He groaned. "I guess..." He sighed and sat down, putting the shoes he'd just searched on. After a moment's thought, he checked the soles. Nothing on there either. Wherever this tracker was, it was hidden very well. The scattered contents of his bag were lying all around but there was nothing suspicious. Perhaps he was wrong about the tracker, but it was probably best to have Aiden over, check the contents of the bag.

He finished tying up his shoes and looked over. "Well then. Let's do this spreadsheet."

Gabrielle grinned. "Gladly." She opened the door for him.

It was dark by the time they got to Twitch's place. Furcifer rang the bell.

"Twitch, it's me. I dumped all my stuff so there's no tracker on me."

"Are you alone?" Twitch asked.

"Yes."

"No." Gabrielle said, staring at Furcifer.

Furcifer groaned and threw his head back. "Fine. Gabrielle's here."

A few minutes of silence. Furcifer was about to try again when he heard Twitch's voice. "You're not coming in."

"Twitch! Come on, seriously? I told you. We need to work together on this."

"No, we don't."

"Open the door!" Furcifer pushed at the door now. But there was no more reply from the other end.

"We can wait for someone to come out." Furcifer took a step back. "And I know where his front door is."

Gabrielle sighed. "I think he's made it abundantly clear that he doesn't want us here."

"Let's wait ten minutes. Let's just - He'll calm down."

"You said that when we left the coffee shop." She sat down on one of the benches and summoned a cigarette. This time, Furcifer didn't even move to stop her. It felt pretty appropriate.

He turned to her when she blew a plume of smoke into the air above.

“What now?”

“He’ll come round. I know it.” He said, looking over.

“You’re too sure about that.” She shivered. “It’s getting cold, let’s go back.”

Furcifer looked at the closed door, defeated.

“Alright.” He said, turning around. The light of the lantern in the courtyard was on fully now - the sun had set completely. He walked over to the street side, blinking when he saw flashing lights. A police car.

It stopped right besides them and two cops in safety vests got out.

Gabrielle stomped out her cigarette and walked over.

“Good evening.” One of the officers started.

“Hi officers, what seems to be the problem?” Furcifer asked, a shiver down his neck. While they looked and acted differently from American officers, speaking to police never had been his favourite thing to do.

“Right, we've had a call that you're refusing to leave the premises and we'd like to sort that out. Can I get your names, please?”

“It’s ok, we’ll leave.” She put a hand on Furcifer’s shoulder. There was a note of something in her voice which he didn’t like.

“Twitch called the cops on us?” He didn’t believe it.

“It's fine. I'm Gabrielle Vaughn.”

“Okay, do you have some ID on you? And you sir?”

“Uh, Atze Furcifer.” He fumbled for his wallet, belatedly realising - he had given up the wrong name. He had travelled under Ronan Johnson and that was the ID he had on him.

The panic that had set in when he heard Gabrielle's beaten voice was only getting harder to control now. This wasn’t just the police telling them to beat it. His mouth went dry as he realised what this was really about. His fingers were sweaty as he thrust out the passport, somehow hoping it would stand up to the scrutiny.

“Ok sir.” One officer opened his passport, and then Gabrielle's. As expected, their eyes just took it in, no reaction. After a second the officer held the passports back out.

“Alright. Sir, this does not match with the data you've just given me. Can you please come with me to the station?”

Chapter 17

Zeus City was always most beautiful at night. Aiden looked around at the row of houses, newly built, stacked between the older houses that were not yet old enough to tear down. They had been maintained wonderfully, either way.

He stubbed out his cigarette as a group of youngsters approached the courtyard, one of them thrusting a camera into his face.

"You're Aiden?" He asked.

Aiden backed away a little. "I am. Put the camera down." He said. "Do you want the neighbours to start thinking weird stuff about what we're doing here?"

He shook his head and collected his fee as they walked in.

"Shhh. I've got a little one upstairs." He said, nodding into the lounge.

"Alright, alright." The teens chuckled and looked over to him. "This is going to be dope."

One wielded an expensive camcorder one they put down in one corner of the room. Aiden shook his head - young men in designer clothing, looking for thrills that wouldn't endanger their trust funds.

Aiden took a deep breath and started making a salt circle, before putting a few objects in a star shape within the salt circle.

"So Aiden, please tell us what you'll be doing?" One of the teenagers licked his lips then turned the camera to Aiden. He looked to be the oldest one, probably hoping to get a good online viral video or something out of this. Aiden glanced up from his work.

"The dæmon you want to summon is dangerous. I hope you know that." He said, looking over before starting to point out the objects.
"To ward us we have the salt circle, sage, a silver pendant of the goddess, a crucifix, the candle to represent the light and the crystal to capture him in." He said, before lighting extra candles.
"No matter what you summon, they'll screw with the electricity. We don't want to end up in pitch blackness when this thing shows."

The boys nodded.
"It'll help us film too." The tallest one carefully readjusted the camera.
"Stop that. Pay attention to what I'm saying." Aiden pointed at the circle. "Stay out of the salt circle, don't touch any of the objects. Just... Don't touch anything and do what I say, whatever it is."
"Alright alright." At least the older boy, a tall jock, seemed to take it somewhat seriously. Aiden nodded at him, appreciating the boy's earnestness. The three others weren't terrible, but they were smirking and chuckling the whole way through. Probably had shared a blunt before coming over. Their reflexes could be slowed. He didn't like that.

"Alright." He took a deep breath and took out an ancient looking tome. "Sawwahdedh. Muuuuuhnicipa. Paairieee." He took a deep breath as he let the vibrations go around before lighting the central candle. The smoke of the candle wisped around in the dimply lit room.

After that he went back to the book.
"Azathoth. Niiyuuuuvehah." He took a deep breath and blinked. "It's here..." He gasped as a brush of air blew out a candle.

"Please, tell us who you are." Aiden droned, as a door slammed shut. Aiden jumped and looked around.
"They like slamming doors. Like teenagers." Aiden chuckled nervously and licked his lips.
"Is this Azeele? Lord of souls?" There was a definite shuffling sound heard behind them, and the hairs on the back of Aiden's neck stood up, before hearing a low growl. A gust of wind blew out a candle. Aiden quickly leaned in to relight it, when he noticed it had disturbed the salt circle line, close to where he sat.
"What... Hand me the sa-" He suddenly tensed up and then doubled up, shoving his hands in the salt circle to keep his balance.
"No- No!" He gasped again and then let out a blood curdling scream. He blinked, his eyes turning fully black.

"Call the constable!" Aiden called out in a high tone before grinning, his rump twisting almost unnaturally. His voice suddenly sounded much deeper, eerier. His eyes had turned fully black.
"Oh, oops, that was the laaast one. Victorian lass, she was delicious!" A snarling laugh resounded in the small lounge. The candle light lit the demonically twisted facial expression, big white teeth grinning.

Suddenly, Oni started crying upstairs.
"BABY!" Aiden grinned, brushing past the petrified teens at an almost inhuman speed.
The jock grabbed the camera and rushed out, soon followed by the rest of his group.
"Let's get the fuck out of here!"
"Don't we need to do some kind of ritual finishing or something?"
"Yeah, tell that to the guy who summoned the thing!" The tallest teenager was already yanking at the door. Another grabbed the camcorder and followed him quickly.

Unseen, Aiden watched them take off from the top of the stairs before laughing and walking over to the nursery to check the little one.
Oni had been a foundling and her innate sense of magic was noticeable even to humans. It was why the police had

contacted him when they had found her. In one fell swoop, Furcifer had made him the one magic shopkeeper, the one magic scholar and a student of magic. He was often contacted first whenever the police in Zeus city noticed anything magical and out of the ordinary. At first he hadn't even thought about adopting her - as a single parent? It would be madness with his schedule. But Jeffrey had encouraged him, and it had been a good decision for them.

"It's okay sweetie." He kissed the top of her head as he peeled out the sclera lenses. These little parties with teenagers thinking they were actually summoning dæmons were a lot of fun for him. It was an easy five hundred, and it gave him a chance to perform again. Honestly he missed doing grand performances but this scratched the itch without starting the whole illusionist shebang again. A few of his "Dæmon summonings" were already online, and he loved the challenge: he had to do them without any magic whatsoever. If he did, it might invite some actual spirit or whatever wanting to play. No, all the effects were practical. It made for a nice, magic free night off.

Russell made his way down the stairs. "They're gone? Quite a calm bunch this time."
"Oh they were running." Aiden grinned, looking over from his boyfriend to the little one in his arms. He would have adopted

the little girl on his own, but to have someone else there who loved her as much was wonderful. It almost... No, it did feel like a family.

Russell chuckled. “She needs her bottle before she can go back to bed.” He took the little one back from the man and kissed his cheek. “I’m always amazed how well you time her crying into your little performance.”

“It’s not a little one! It requires serious planning, strenuous research, and a lot of practice.” He groaned. He’d pulled a muscle doing his snake move and he was sure he was developing a bruise from having fallen onto the pot of salt.

“Yes yes yes.” Russell rolled his eyes. “You put a lot more effort into that than into your uni life.”

“Well.” Shrugged Aiden. “One night off doesn’t hurt anyone and it makes good money.”

“It does.” Russell had to admit. It was a good way to make their grocery bill.

“And I’m not failing my courses, or skimping out on classes. I’m guessing I’ve already taught more classes than Furcifer

did when he was teaching."
"That can't be hard." Russell walked to the kitchen and started up a bottle for the baby. "Do you miss him?"
Aiden frowned as he thought about it. To be honest he hadn't given his relationship with the mage much thought since he had left. He'd had to get on with things.
"Of course I do." He finally said with a little shrug. "He was a friend. But he made his choice..."

No, Aiden greatly preferred his own life with Russell. The shop was not making as much money anymore, but with Russell tending it and he himself teaching at university, they made ends meet easily. The one issue was that they weren't exactly saving up enough to make a college fund for the little one.

Oh he knew, one call and she would be in the Canutta program, if only because they would want to observe how a little one born with magic would thrive. It was theorised a person needed about a year to master their skills to a basic level, but for Oni that would probably be a lot shorter. The Canutta school would enlist her in their schools until she was eighteen, then send her to the finest university, fully funded. Besides that he still had standing in the magic community - his neutrality and the excellent quality of his magical goods kept people coming back. He had even been invited to the table to discuss the new magic laws.

And he had been thinking about sending her to a magic school more and more. Of course he could teach her a few things. How to work out her natural talent, figure out what she was good at. But that wasn't what she needed. She would be more powerful than most mages at a younger age and would need proper schooling.

"You're thinking about the schools again aren't you?" Russell piped up.
"You can't say it hasn't crossed your mind after we spent the weekend camping outside a preschool only to be turned away." Aiden sighed and stroked the head of the little one.
"Of course it has." Russell looked down to the bottle and sighed. "It... might be good for her. But I don't want her to

turn out like... that."
"You mean like Furcifer?"
"Like someone who can create a thunderstorm but has no idea how to apologise to a friend." Russell looked over to him.
"It's just a backup for now. There's a few other schools we can try." Aiden said as he took the formula from him.
"And it shouldn't be more than a back up." Said Russell.
"I know, I know." He looked over, a little frustrated. Russell was kind but he had no idea how the magic world worked.

"But I just... think it's something to keep in mind." Aiden wouldn't mind her getting a free ride just for being magical. At the same time he knew that she would grow to learn a lot of their philosophy. It might even lead people to believe his neutrality had been compromised. With a sigh he looked over to his phone.
"He actually texted back." Aiden raised an eyebrow.
Russell sighed. "Don't even bother with him... You know it'll end badly."

"Yes, perhaps... " Aiden sighed, frustrated. Part of him hated that he was at odds with the man. Furcifer had been a friend for so long. But he couldn't help but feel betrayed - only a few years ago, despite his protests, Furcifer had taken a leadership position at a Faction.
For many, many reasons Aiden could never be a part of that

world. It was very likely one of the Factions had caused the death of his wife.

Even the fact that he was invited to the talks frustrated him a little.

“Did you see the broadcast from the IMG?” Aiden asked, looking over.

“Of course I did.” Russell said. “Is that why you texted Furcifer?”

“Yeah. He and Gabrielle could be in big trouble.” Though secretly he was happy about it. Perhaps the factions would finally fall apart now, be exposed for the shambling mess they were. It was unlikely - the factions had been around for a while and they had only continued to grow.

“I know. But what if they really tortured that man?”

“Gabrielle did torture that man. It was... Shushed and Twitch disappearing only helped in their favour. But if they want to make things right they need to face what they did, and what they condoned. I don't even know why you're surprised.”

Russell shook his head. “I guess I'm not after Jeffrey... ”

The man's roommate had died alone in a cell as a result of Furcifer. It was not a happy thought for either of them.

Russell sighed. “I think you’d best stay out of this mess.” He ran a hand through his hair. In Aiden’s arms, Oni calmed down and started settling in to sleep. Hopefully she would sleep through the rest of the night.

"Furcifer did ask for my help on this case." Perhaps his own fault. He had reached out, but that didn't mean he could not refuse to help, right?

"I would be careful, Ai. That man has a tendency to destroy whoever is around him."

"I know." Aiden said, shaking his head before getting up to put the baby back down. This argument would go in circles. But then and there he made a decision. He tucked the baby in and turned to Russell.

"I'll just call him tomorrow morning to see what's going on. That's all." He said and put his hands up.

Russell sighed. "You're too good. I'm going to bed."

Aiden doubted that he was very good.

In fact when morning came, he had forgotten all about calling Furcifer back.

Chapter 18

Furcifer felt... As if his feet weren't quite touching the ground. Like the world around him was not real. They passed by the grey walls of the police station, slowly walking towards the exit with an officer guiding them.
Fact, Twitch had called the police on them.
Fact, Gabrielle and he had been arrested.

Gabrielle touched his arm. They'd been told they were free to go, for now. They would have to remain available to the police and return to Zeus City as soon as they had concluded their business here. So for now there would be no arrests, and after he had explained the passport mishap and got a distressed intern to bring over the real passport through an authorised portal, they were free to go.

In all fairness the case against them wasn't very strong. Twitch had not filed a formal complaint and the Guild had very little of a case without properly describing the notebook.

In a haze he remembered what his lawyers had told him over the phone.
There would likely be no case around the notebook. Gabrielle, however, could be in trouble if the Guild convinced Twitch to press charges and he had no idea whether or not they had spoken to him. Interpol had a blue notice out on them, for information. They had given that information so there should be no issues, if no charges were pressed.

Either way, that was all easy for them to say from the safety of their boardroom, on speakerphone.
Finally, the final door opened and they were in the street.
"We can get you a ride." The police officer looked over, but Furcifer shook his head. He was just about done being around uniformed men, worrying that whatever he said could get them into even deeper trouble.
"Let's go." Said Gabrielle. Her voice was almost hoarse, a sign she was exhausted.
He nodded, too exhausted to portal straight to their room. Lazily he put an arm up and hailed a cab.

As he settled into the strange smelling cab, he made a face. It had been a while since he had actually been inside a taxi. It was clean, though the interior looked worn.
"Where to?"
It took Furcifer a moment before he could recite the

address.
"Alrighty." The driver turned on the meter and started driving. In the relative darkness of the cab, Furcifer sat back, the light of the streetlights reflecting inside.
Gabrielle stared ou. He couldn't imagine what was going on inside her head right now.
"I'm screwed, aren't I?" She suddenly broke the silence.
"Mmmm? No. Look. Twitch isn't going to..."
"You know, I could have believed that before he called the cops on us." She cut him off. "Right now, all bets are off. I'm surprised he didn't already file charges." She sounded sullen and defeated.
"Perhaps. But right now there's not much we can do." He said.
After what seemed like forever, she nodded and looked over. "So what now?"
The hoarse note in her voice was back.

"We act alone. If we get enough of the books, neither of them can do much with them." From what Twitch had told him, he would be destroying the books. But they were pretty valuable as a resource. If at all possible, Furcifer wanted to save them. Display them.

She cleared her throat. "I figured out where the next one is." She looked over. "I found some correspondence from Etta to friends. She went to the United Kingdom at some point, perhaps because Twitch -" She made a gesture. He got it. Twitch was originally from here, so it was not unlikely she had come here to do research on his roots.

"And?" He was eager to keep her talking. It kept her from sounding completely defeated.

"Look. One's in the sewers. Not going anywhere near that and I think nobody's found that one yet." He took a deep breath. "The other was given away as a gift when it was first found." He cleared his throat.

"I can find that one. Not to worry." He looked over. "I promise. But you have to say you'll come with me to find it."

She frowned. "Yeah. Sure. But I'm not coming near Twitch."

He took a deep breath. There was no way to tell he wouldn't be there. If Twitch had followed the same leads, he would be there as well.

"Anyway. We'll figure that out when we get there." The car pulled over and he pushed the door open, shivering as the cold night air hit.

The lights inside the flat were still on. Furcifer glanced over to Gabrielle - they had turned the lights off to make sure the bug, if it had a video element, it could not see anything in the room.

Gabrielle swallowed and opened the door carefully.

The room was a mess - the bedding had been pulled off of the beds, the table was swiped clean and all drawers had been ransacked. Luckily, he had cast his non-detection spell on the envelope with his notes in it.

"Thank goodness. It's still here." He sighed. His notes on the books - he was so glad he'd remembered to lock them away.

"Did they get anything?" Gabrielle craned her neck.

"No." He shook his head. "Well, if they did it's nothing important."

She nodded. "Maybe they wanted to retrieve their... "

The bug. He shook his head. "I doubt it." He said, hoping she got the message. He didn't want to mention the bug, in case somehow the people behind planting the bug had no idea that they knew. A cursory check of his phone showed him that Aiden had not replied, so it looked like they were on their own for this one.

Well, he might as well take some time and find the damn thing then. He put a finger to his mouth. Immediately, she seemed to understand. She reached out for the clothes he'd worn earlier and ran her hands over the fabric. He grabbed his messenger bag and emptied it in the floor.

Notebooks, pens, napkins and a wallet fluttered down to the ground.

Gabrielle and he were doing it again, dancing around one another. There was a beautiful, eerie familiarity in how they moved in an almost synchronous way. Their hands touched, and they glanced at each other - but it only lasted a second.

He looked around and grabbed the jeans he'd been wearing, patting them vigorously. Finally - he found it.

On top of the fly's button was a layer of... Something. It looked brassy and embossed, and it came off of the top of the button easily. He glanced over to Gabrielle and she nodded to the bathroom.

He walked over to the bathroom and flushed it.

"I think that was it." He sighed. It felt like a huge relief.

"Eww. They were listening in on your junk." She laughed. It was a small victory but it had come just in time. Gabrielle was smiling again for the first time since they had set foot in this place.

“Yeah.” He grinned a little. “At least that’s sorted.” He chuckled at the thought of them following the trail of the bug, down the sewers.

“So this plan of yours.”

“We’re breaking in and stealing the notebook.”

Her grip on her phone tensed so hard he worried he could hear it cracking.

“I’m sorry, what?”

Chapter 19

Furcifer poured himself another cup of coffee. After a quiet night's sleep they both seemed to need badly at this moment, he had explained his plan better.

"It'll be easy, we just break in at night..."

She held a hand out. "Those are already two very bad ideas." She got up and put some milk in her coffee. "You don't just break in at night, that's the most stupid idea. Not to mention we've just been released by the police after questioning - getting caught breaking in will end us in jail."

He sighed. "There was another option."

"Come on. Tell me." She sipped the coffee, staring over to him.

"The owners are throwing a party. Tonight."

She grinned widely. "Now that's a much better plan." She said. "We can go shop for some threads."

"I -" He sighed. "It's in their private library. It'll probably be hard to find."

"I like a challenge. Also, shopping." She put the mug down

and slipped into her low heeled shoes. "Come on. Can't drop that on a girl then go back on your word. Also, who are the owners?"
"Well... Dean, I mean former Dean, Mara Terry. She is uh, she used to be the dean at the university I worked at."
She nodded. "And you have no issues stealing from her?"
"Nope."
"Then let's go shopping."
Furcifer laughed. "Okay, but first... I want to go see Twitch. Just... Make sure he's okay."
Gabrielle sighed. "Go now then. I'll finish up here and meet you in Oxford Circus or one of those posh shopping streets. I'll just text you where I am when you're done."
He got up and walked to the bathroom.
"Thanks, Gab." He said. She seemed to understand - and be a lot more at ease. It looked like things were finally looking up for them. He put his shoes on and walked outside, catching a taxi to Twitch's flat.

It looked very different in the light of day, or maybe he had just not taken the time to take in the old stonework.
He walked over to the doorbells, this time finding Twitch's name easily, and rang the doorbell.

After a tense thirty seconds, there was no reply. That was awkward. He licked his lips and looked around, wondering if he could tailgate behind someone through the communal door.

"Can I help you?" He didn't recognise the lady behind him. She had reddish blonde hair in a high ponytail and was holding a large stack of document folders in her arms. Somehow she only barely managed to peek over them which probably worked in his favour.

"Oh! Uh, I'm looking for Asa Ward."

"Ah. He's not here right now. I am just feeding his cat."

"Do you know where he went?"

"Eh? No, not really. Oh thanks!" She slipped in as someone opened the door to leave. He briefly considered following her in, but then shook his head. The last thing he needed was to have to police called on him twice in a twenty four hour period.

"Alright, have a good day!" He called after her as the door closed.

That had been a waste of time. Looked like he had left to find the next notebook. He sighed and checked his phone as he walked. There had still been no response from Alyce Cole - it seemed she had not taken his suggestion to take the name to the police. Well, he would deal with that later. He put his phone away and walked off, unaware he had been observed from behind dainty, lacy little curtains.

Chapter 20

Twitch had heard the exchange outside and opened his door for Lydia.

"Was it him?"

"Redhead, looks a bit like a crappy vampire, couldn't act casual if his life depended on it? Yeah."

He chuckled at that description. "Thanks for this." He said, looking over the stack of paperwork she had brought in.

"You're welcome... though why are you hiding from your friends? And what's all this?" She gestured at the papers.

He'd found it was easiest to keep the notes he had in school - there was a locked drawer, security cameras, and it was close by him during most of his working day.

"I'm looking for something." He said. There was a moment of silence in which Twitch wondered whether to explain it, but suddenly she broke the silence, fidgeting with her fingers. He could feel that tension again, and a few of the pages of the pile started floating.

"Argh! I'm sorry!" She gasped and pushed them down. "I'm so sorry. Stuff's been... doing that around me and..." She blushed. It was the first time he'd heard her put it into words.

"You're exhibiting signs of untamed, unreleased magic. How long has it been manifesting like that?" He said without looking up from the notes he was sorting out.

Her eyes went wide and he looked up briefly. He had obviously touched on something there. Both of them had had some training for the school on how to deal with kids who had magic, but it was pretty superficial. It had been the initiative of an educator who had some experience with magic education but nothing too far reaching. Nothing dealing with how magic came to manifest in a person. That kind of knowledge wasn't exactly spread far and wide.

"You think so? Uh, six months. How do you know all this? I'm pretty sure magic awareness training didn't cover any of this."

"Of course it didn't. It was rudimentary at best." He scoffed and closed the folder. For a moment it was quiet as he thought about how to explain it best.

"Kids aren't born with magic. It happens. It seems to be some sort of external factor that triggers some kind of gene, or changes a part of the brain structure. It's not gmo's, it's not global warming. It's... benevolent." He walked over to her and made one of the paper folders float up, before opening and closing it and landing it back onto the rest of the pile of paper. Gothball's behind wiggled before jumping onto the tower.

"You have magic?" He was sure she had never seen a person with such powers.

"Yes. I've got some talent and I've been studying these things." He said. "I can maybe even speed up the process for you. Usually people can come into their power comfortably within three months, four at most. If it is taking so long you may need a nudge. Metaphorically speaking."

She looked down at her own hands, trembling slightly as she was trying to process this.

"So.... What now?" She asked, mind still reeling. "I mean. I

have so many questions. What - How come if you're magic you're teaching a-level history rather than teaching... well, spells and stuff and what can I do, is it like an unlimited power or do I have to recharge?"
"Because I like history, you do have unlimited power if you train it well but it depends on your own stamina. You can train it to get better and more efficient at it, but at some point you will be exhausted. As for what to do now, give me your hands."

He held his own hands out slightly, waiting for her to cross the distance. This was important and she would have to take the biggest step forward.
She flexed her fingers momentarily before taking his hands and looking up towards him.

"They're warm." She smiled a little.
He nodded and then looked into her eyes. "Okay. I'm just sending some magic through to your hands. No, nothing bad. It's a little bit of warming magic, like the same I use to warm my hands. It'll hopefully jump start your power so you can come into it properly and start learning how to use it."
"Okay." She put her hands back and looked up to him. "I trust you." She said, sounding grave.
"And I won't do anything to lose that trust. Ready?" He maintained the eye contact.

She nodded shakily. "Ready." She agreed and took a deep breath, releasing it slowly as Twitch sent a soft pulse of energy downwards.

It felt as if she was suddenly handed a warm hand warmer. Within a few seconds, the warmth travelled through her body. It was definitely having some sort of effect on her. She let out a deep breath and dropped her hands by her side.

She opened her eyes again and looked at Twitch.

"I think..." She sounded hoarse and had to clear her throat before continuing.

"I think that did it." She said softly, looking to the table and raising her hand. Nothing happened to the plate she was pointing at.

"It doesn't work!" She frowned.

"Oh, no, only instinctual magic works that way. Instinctual magic is like... background radiation. It isn't very effective and really only like... your aura." He explained. "To actually use your power, you're going to need spells until you're good enough at it that you can do without." He walked to the book case and sought out one of Furcifer's published spellbooks.

"That should help you underway. But for now it should keep your chicken nuggets on your plate."

"This... is even more studying than I've already had to do to get my job?"

"Everything worth something in life requires studying for

some time." He shrugged. "If you want you can not study and just learn intuitively, but it takes a lot longer than you would imagine."

"Huh..." She took the book and sighed, flicking through it. "So, do I learn to write spells with this as well?"

"Not explicitly, but most logical people figure out how spells are built up.

"There is a university course on magic in Zeus City which helps a lot of people, but I think this book will already give you ninety percent of what you need for daily life." He had read a lot about Aiden's magic course online and much like Furcifer's, there was a large focus on history of magic and spell writing, though most mages never really got to that level anyway. It was much like crochet - many people, including Twitch, were happy to either play around with basic ways of making different things or followed a pattern. It was only quite advanced crafters who ended up writing and publishing patterns.

Lydia nodded at that. "So... you only use magic at home?"

"Yeah. I know there's more and more magic users coming out, but I'm not really...ready to join that movement yet. I'm just doing my own thing, I guess."

"I like that." She nodded. "But there are like organisations?"

"Yep. I'll put a good word in for you at some of them. You can do some research first. They're a bit like political parties and

they all have their own outlook on things." He said. "They're called factions."
"Thanks for this." She held the book up. "Can I take it home?"
"Of course." Twitch said. He only briefly looked up from the papers. It was a lot, he knew, so he wanted to leave her with that. Right now he would have preferred to spend more time with her to teach her things, but time was short. Without Furcifer on his side things had just gotten a lot more difficult.

Besides, he knew where the next book was.
"I need to go. I need to go pick something up." He said.
"Can I come?"
"No, I don't think that's a good idea." He said. "I'm sorry. I'll explain later." He grabbed his coat. "You can stay here if you want, go through the books. I just... need to go get something. I should be back soon."
She made a face and sighed. "I'll see you tomorrow then." She walked up and pecked his lips. It was a soft touch. But he could feel her soft lips brush his own before she left the flat.

Twitch momentarily forgot all he had been doing. It took him a few minutes to remember why he was standing there with a coat in one hand.

Chapter 21

Twitch said his goodbyes to Lydia then walked down the stairs into the underground station. After walking through an empty hall, he looked around and leaned against a maintenance door, slipping in easily with the help of a spell. The CCTV cameras didn't cover this part of the station, so he was not worried about being caught. The hardest part was actually breaching the doors as they were quite solidly built and the locks often rusted in place. It had not taken long to do his research about this place, most of these stations were well-documented.

As soon as he was through the door, Twitch walked into the maintenance hallway and flicked on his torch before consulting the map he had found in one of the notebooks.
"Left, left... over the catwalk then to the right." He nodded and started off. Somehow, speaking to himself was helping in this situation. It was not breaking in. He was just walking through a rarely used hallway, nothing more. And as soon as he had the book he would be right out of here. He continued

to the first left, then took another left. The walls of the maintenance tunnel were smoothly tiled, but encrusted with filth and graffiti. There were lamps mounted to the walls, but turning them on would probably trigger some sort of alert, so Twitch relied on a torch to find his way around. After about a hundred meters, he came to a catwalk, a high bridge over the tracks. It had been mentioned in the clues, so he knew he at least had not gotten lost.

He breathed a sigh of relief. The catwalk's state quickly turned his mood though - it was not very sturdy looking. He put a careful step onto the bridge and took a deep breath. It was a good thing he was not very burly. Cautiously, he moved his other foot in front of his first, and then grabbed the handrail. Bad decision - he squeaked as he touched a rat which scurried away.

"Gross..." He reached into his bag for hand sanitizer when he heard the bridge groan under his weight. Perhaps not the best time to worry about germs.

"Gotta keep going gotta keep going..." He grabbed the handrail with more conviction and hurried over. No time for cleanliness, time to keep moving. A sound was echoing through the tunnel and it worried him. If he had known exactly where he was going he could have used a spell, but it was too dangerous. It was too easy to teleport into a wall or something. And he was hearing a strange, low sound which he hoped was just construction works going on down the line.

Once he had crossed the catwalk, he took a deep breath. Just in front of him there was a little breaker box. He opened it up easily and found what he was looking for - a notebook, neatly wrapped in plastic wrap.
"Ah, wonderful." He put the book away and took a few steps back towards the catwalk. This time however, the first step broke as soon as he tried to put weight on it. He scraped his ankle, not having been fast enough to draw his foot back in time. Pulling back, he fell backwards into the breaker box. Ugh! His heart was racing. He would have to find another way out. Hopefully, there would be another catwalk just a few hundred meters down.

As he calmed down, he noticed the sound was growing stronger. It was... a thumping sound, but so frequent it sounded like... scurrying. He went wide eyed and started running. Fuck! He turned the torch to try and find the source of the sound. A large shadow moved across the wall of the tunnel beyond the bridge. Twitch froze as the being came into view - a large spider, about six feet high, moved into view, roaring fiercely at the mage beyond. Despite the lack of eyes, it easily homed in on Twitch.

It must be the notebook, Twitch realised as he looked at the large being. It would have been impossible not to have heard the large being in the tunnels, and he had barely heard it before removing the book. It had to be some kind of guardian.

The lidded body stopped, the head raised up to the roof. It wielded two large pincers, and the huge legs were covered in coarse looking hair.
Twitch took a deep breath. He had to act here before the being reached the bridge. Breathing out, he started a freezing spell. The spider seemed based on an exotic specimen so it was not far fetched to assume it was susceptible to cold. The cold tingled in his fingers, before a large, freezing vapour extended from his digits. As it hurled towards the spider it became a large cone of ice.

As Twitch expected, the spider backed away from it. One leg was caught in the blast, the tip of it frozen to the wall. With a mighty roar, the creature pulled loose and rushed forward towards the bridge.

Twitch sighed a breath of relief. There was no way the bridge would hold the spider's weight. It was stuck there.

Meanwhile the spider eyed up the bridge then scurried onto the wall, avoiding the bridge entirely as it walked on the ceiling.

"Oh shit!" Twitch quickly shot out another spell, but then turned and ran before checking if it had even hit. He had to focus - one wrong turn and he would be lost in these tunnels. One of the spider's legs grazed his own and he gasped as it tripped him up. He twisted, kicked at the being's head, and moved back. No good - he could barely outrun it. He relaunched the cold spell and fired it at the floor, making it slippery. The cold spells were taking their toll, though. He could feel his fingers freezing - a painful tingling feeling leaving his skin red. He breathed warm air on it and ran, looking back to see the spider slipping on the ice. It wouldn't stop it for long, though.

One left, one right - he found himself in front of a dead end.

"Crap." He turned his back to the wall and closed his eyes, hearing the cursed scurrying move closer.

Chapter 22

The former dean dodged a caterer and continued through to the kitchen. A brief retreat from the party, albeit short lived.

Mara pushed open the door to the kitchen and paused to pour herself a glass of water, looking over the caterer's plates set out, ready to be taken out to the lounge.

Only the best of course- plates of sushi, delightful seafood canapes and crunchy mini quiches. She picked up one of the quiches and popped it into her mouth with a satisfied groan.

Her fundraiser was going well. Turnout was high and people were giving - many donations had been agreed upon and the talks given by herself and a few educators she had invited had gone down well... Her hope was that she would finally be able to launch a proper program from magic in schools and to hire some mages to instruct teachers in dealing with magical children.

She herself was not magic. She didn't think she would be a late bloomer at it, either. It didn't make a difference to her. Because of the magic classes at her university she had grown to care about the budding community. There had been very little in Zeus City, but returning to the UK she had found there was even less. She had set up the magic awareness training programme for teachers - all of whom were likely to come into contact with mages at some point during their careers. One of the keynote lectures had been on the positive feedback they had received from teachers about it.

"Get out there." She whispered to herself, taking a deep breath before putting a smile back on her face and walking out to the crowd.
"Miss Terry!" A mage she recognised as Ethan, from the IMG, hailed her and she walked straight over. She was partial to him - he had a boyish charm and unlike most of his guild he was quite open. In short, he was the kind of man she'd happily ask out for some coffee. Especially in that tuxedo.

"Ethan!" She smiled. "So glad you could make it. Is Quentin with you?"
"Oh, sadly not, but he sent the thing that matters the most with me - his cheque book."
Mara couldn't help but chuckle. "I'm sure he's very busy." She probed a little. Like most people even remotely interested

in magic she had kept up with the coverage of the IMG's recent press conference.

"He is. He is." Ethan said, sipping a glass of champagne. "It's a tricky situation, obviously."

"Obviously." She waved away a tray of champagne. Never had been a drinker, her. Even though Furcifer had almost driven her to it sometimes.

"I'm glad to see the IMG support our initiative. The donation Quentin agreed to is... substantial."

"Of course. As an international faction we want to support all of our members."

And future ones, she thought. If the IMG had their name displayed on any of the materials handed to teachers, it would be the only known faction for a lot of them. Even so, they were still here - which was more than she could say of the other factions she had sent invites to.

Granted, many did not have chapters outside of Zeus City. Not yet.

"I'm glad to hear." She said, realising she'd been quiet for too long.

"In fact, we'd like to discuss sponsorship."

And here we go, she thought. The real agenda.

"We don't want to just give some money here and now but to make long term contributions. Your organisation is only just getting on its feet, and we'd love to support that."

“I... had not thought of that yet.” She fibbed, looking over, yet again waving away a tray of champagne. It was starting to irritate her, though that could be because she thought she could see a familiar mop of red hair among the crowd.

“I would have to give it thought, but I would welcome the support.” She had to admit. So far she had not gotten any funds from the government and her fundraising efforts were only getting her so far. However it seemed dangerous to take a side when there was an obvious struggle between the IMG and the Elites.

“Excuse me one second.” She raised a finger and chased after the spot of red in the crowd.

“Atze Furcifer.” She grinned and looked over. “And I was hoping retirement would save me from ever having to deal with you.”

“Oh! Dean - mean, Miss Terry.”

“You’re responsible for half of the grey hairs on my head, Atze. I think we’re on a first name basis.” She had been the dean at the university where he had taught his first lectures on magic. Suffice to say he had been one of the biggest challenges in her career.

Furcifer seemed to wince at the use of his first name, a fact she delighted in.
"I would have expected Gabrielle, rather than you."
"And miss this party? No way."
"You didn't RSVP." She replied drily. "I mean, Gabrielle agreed to a donation but... "

"Well you know how it goes. One day you're leading a faction and the other you're on the run cause of accusations of torture." Gabrielle popped up behind him. "We should go."
"You can't leave. Have you donated yet?" Said Mara, finding herself a lot more direct with Furcifer.
"Oh!" Strangely enough, it seemed like Gabrielle only now seemed to realise she was at a fundraising event.
"Yes. The IMG is writing down an amount right now." She motioned to Ethan who was indeed filling in a donation book at one of the little tables.
"I heard him mention a five zero number." She said innocently.
Gabrielle's eyes narrowed and she furiously sought in her small party purse for her chequebook.

"Please, please. I'll handle this." Furcifer walked away for a second. His gait was a bit stiff - she wondered if he had chosen too tight a cummerbund. After a few minutes he came back with an envelope - pilfered from her writing table in the downstairs office.

"I am sure this will meet your approval." He said, manner dignified as ever. "Unfortunately, we should go. I don't think it's a good idea for us to be in the same room as the IMG right now. It was great to see you."

She nodded and took the envelope he held out. "Likewise, Furcifer." She said, watching them walk off.

As soon as they were out of sight, she opened the envelope, curious to see if her deceit had worked.
With a groan she read the note inside.

In red ink, he had scribbled on the paper:

I O U

An amount with 5 0s

xx

Furcifer

Chapter 23

Gabrielle had to admit the dean had done well for herself. The house she had in this neighbourhood was stunning and rather large.

After ditching Furcifer as a distraction she had made her way up the stairs.
There was no security to speak of, and even if there was someone she was prepared to deal with it. Faster than anyone on stiletto heels ought to be, she climbed the stairs and rushed down the hall towards Mara's private study.

It was a lucky guess - the first door she had opened had turned out to be the woman's office.
It was a modern affair, with a large window, covered with blinds, and a large white desk offset with an old fashioned office chair, the leather cracking with age. Gabrielle liked it. The juxtaposition was so carefree, so different from the rest of the painstakingly modern and beautifully furnished house.

Or perhaps she didn't want to decorate this because it was her personal space. With a shiver, Gabrielle realised not for the first time that night she was an intruder. She licked her lips and walked behind the desk.

Without any visible security and no magic to speak of, this would be easy. She just needed to locate the book. After briefly searching the desk's drawers, she turned to the bookshelves.

She ran a finger over the spines as she walked and read the titles. Most were works on education, but there were more and more books about magic. She really was robbing one of the good guys here.

Former dean Mara Terry had lobbied to the Elites for funding for her programme, and she had agreed on a civilised amount. Not much, but something to keep her going, really. With the Scribes planning on their own schools, there seemed to be little need to help other educational programmes.

"Aha!" She grinned as her eyes fell on a familiar style cover. "There we go..." She took the book and put it away behind her small purse, almost folding it in half to make it fit. She walked down the stairs again and rejoined Furcifer, shoving the book under his jacket, into the back of his cummerbund.

"Well you know how it goes. One day you're leading a faction and the other you're on the run cause of accusations of torture." Gabrielle smiled and looked to Furcifer. "We should go."
"You can't leave. Have you donated yet?" Said Mara.

Gabrielle sighed, suddenly a lot less sorry about the theft now that it looked like Mara wasn't going to let them go without an extra donation. I suppose she could call it a fair deal considering she had spent years with Furcifer. She opened up her purse but Furcifer interrupted. She could not help but breathe a sigh of relief now that this would be handled. Her frantic search for the chequebook stopped.

Furcifer took off and Gabrielle chuckled nervously, hoping he was not about to do something stupid. He returned moments later, and took her arm.
"I am sure this will meet your approval." He said, manner dignified as ever. "Unfortunately, we should go. I don't think it's a good idea for us to be in the same room as the IMG right now. It was great to see you."

Gabrielle took a deep breath as they left. "I got it."
"I could tell. You just shoved it in there." He whispered, trying to walk casually despite the heavy book shoved into his waistband.

Chapter 24

Down in the sewers, Twitch opened his eyes again only to find the spider was still there. A drop of water hit him on the head and he shivered. This could not be how it ended. No. He could not let this thing eat him. He was not going to go down without a fight. Not in some damn sewers! Still, it was approaching fast and he had no idea what to do.

“Focus.” He whispered to himself. It would be no use to lose his wits now. He had launched quite a few magic spells while running, and if he didn’t pace himself he would faint. Right now he reckoned he had about one or two spells left before fatigue would make him useless.

He stared at the thing appearing in his sight. There was something off about the beast. It did not make sense. Like a child had made a drawing of a spider. In fact, it looked exactly how he thought a tarantula would look like. Down to the pincers drooping venom. The ground shook slightly with every step of the being, but the familiarity was too strong. Finally, he recognised it. The spider looked exactly like a drawing in a book he had read once, very long ago. He could remember the book better now - it was one with big pictures. Grey and red. Setting his brother in his lap as they tried to read it together until Etta called them for dinner.

"You are not real." He blinked. "You would have frozen in this tunnel. You would never find enough food to stay alive here. You cannot exist." He took a deep breath and tried to put one leg in front of the other to walk towards the being.
"Don't exist, don't exist..." He stepped forward and stopped a step short of the being. At this range he could see the hairs on its legs, the eyes reflecting his face. The creature raised its front paws in an attack pose, coming up high enough to touch Twitch's head. He quickly closed his eyes again. That was a lot better.

"You don't exist." He took a deep breath and took another step, fully expecting to collide with a leg at this point. But the impact did not come. He opened one eye and spied around for the beast, but it was gone

"Phew..." He took another deep breath and sagged against the wall of the cave. He needed to get out of here now - there was no telling what other traps the witch had set up to avoid the wrong person taking the spell. Now that there was no imminent danger, he took a moment to take in his surroundings. Okay, so he had lost track of where he was during the running. That was something he could amend. He took out his phone to try and figure out where he was, but there was no coverage down here. After a few useless taps he put it away and took out his torch and his own notebook. Torch between his lips he flicked through the pages. No spell to help him out of this mess. The closest thing he had was a spell to direct him to the nearest restroom, and he wasn't sure it wouldn't mistake the sewer for one. The only resource he had left was the book he had just picked up.

He probably should not use it. There were too many unknown factors. But he had to get out of here. If he randomly wandered he could possibly find an exit, right? He looked around. His phone would die in less than an hour. His torch could probably last a bit longer than that but if both died he would be unable to read any spell. Okay, he would check out the newly found notebook. If there was nothing in there he would try his lavatory spell. He slipped the torch back between his teeth and perused the notebook. Onion dicing. No. Magical grocery lists. No. Getting grass stains out of silk. Ugh! He closed the book and took out his own again. Lavatory it was.

Before he could start the spell, he heard a splash behind him. Had the spider reappeared? It was very possible for the spell to reset itself every hour or so to make sure that the hiding place was protected even if one guardian was vanquished. He took a deep breath and turned around.
"Twitch!"
"Ethan!" He was quite surprised to see Ethan, standing in front of him. "What... How did you get here?"
"I was in London so I thought I might as well drop by." He smirked and leaned against the wall, before making a face and trying to wipe down his tuxedo. "Don't worry, I used a spider web portal. Phew! I know London rents are insane but I hope you're not paying too much for this." He grinned boyishly.

Twitch shook his head with a chuckle.

A spider web portal was an advanced technique - it meant the portal created different pathways through the length of it. Only the first person through was able to take the fastest path through to the destination, everyone after it would be lead to dead ends and other destinations. And if you had no idea where the first person through the portal wanted to go, it was quite tricky to trace.

"I brought the book Etta gave me. I think she wanted us both to work on this." Ethan said, more seriously this time.

Twitch bit his lip pensively. After burning the bridge with Furcifer, he could use the help. Contacting Aiden was another possibility. But for now, Ethan's presence would be good.

"I - uh, let's get out of here. I was just about to use a spell to lead us to the nearest lavatory and hopefully, the world above."

"Lead the way." Ethan grinned, looking a bit amused.

Twitch snorted. "Gross. You're way too excited for that."

Ethan chuckled, then looked in his pockets.

"Mum said to give this to you when it was time." He said, handing over an ancient looking, yellowed envelope.

Chapter 25

Gabrielle's slinky dress lay like a puddle on the floor of their safe house, the beads reflecting the morning sun as the shower ran. Yet while any other man would have strained his neck to try and catch a glimpse of her, Furcifer was deeply engrossed in another treasure.

Sipping on a cup of tea, Furcifer read through the notebook stolen from Mara. The dedication on the first page gave him a slight pang of guilt:

Dear Mara,
I know you are done with academia but have fun pouring over this one. Found it around the same time as that bangle so I'm sure it's nothing but trouble, just the way you like it.
Have a wonderful time in England and pop by the museum anytime,
Donnovan

Donnovan – he had been the museum curator he had dealt with before. What a shame. If he didn't have to destroy the book he would return it to her after this was all done.
Even though he had not located the actual part of the Spell, there was a wealth of other spells in here which had not been seen in ages, or had never been found in writing. Even with only the one book, there was a lot of indexing to do. He wanted to sort these spells by effect, harmfulness and duration. He had concluded that the book consisted of maybe twenty percent real spells, the rest being just generated nonsense. This one looked somewhat older though. It had very old fashioned text decorations on some pages, which seemed to have been spliced in. One of the pages was decorated with the image of a man in a forest, digging a hole while he had a book lying at his feet. Perhaps some sort of allusion to how the book was best off hidden away? His eyes darted over it, following the intricate brown lines on the tan paper. There had to have been a reason to splice this in. Or maybe, a fraud art seller had just added them in later to make the book look like more of an antique.

"Gabrielle! Can I call Manon in on this one? She would love this so much!" He called out and leaned back in his seat so he could try and see Gabrielle.
Gabrielle sighed, drying herself off with towel. "Sure. Your friend can come over and play." She snorted. "If you make

sure she doesn't give anyone any clue what we're working on."
"She can handle this." He leaned forward again to look for his phone.
"I don't know if our budget can handle this, Furcifer. We've done nothing but spend money since getting here and for what?"
"For something good, Gabrielle."

He did love Gabrielle, but spending all his waking time with her was starting to take its toll. He could tell she was being shorter and more sarcastic, and he was just withdrawing deeper into the books. Which was probably how he had gotten the idea to start categorising them all.
Gabrielle thought a minute then shrugged. "Yeah, fine. I'm going to go out for the day anyway... Oh your phone has been buzzing."
"Huh! Where is it?" He stood up, said said realising the phone was not under any of the papers on his desk.
Gabrielle put down the plate with a sigh then brought him his phone.
"You left it charging in the kitchen." She said, as Furcifer unlocked it.
"Three missed calls..." He sighed and pushed a button to call back the number.

"Hi. This is Atze Furcifer. I missed a few calls from this number?" He sat back a bit as he heard the person on the other end of the line looking through some papers.
"Ah! Yes, mr Furcifer! This is Beta Airlines, we're happy to inform you your luggage has been found." The southern voice was pleasant, but he could tell there was no real joy in it. Ah, a true call centre worker.
"Luggage? You mean..." He raised an eyebrow as he tried to recall the last time he had lost baggage on this specific airline. "You mean the bags you lost two years ago."
"Just the one bag, actually." The call centre lady said nervously.
"Of course." Furcifer pinched the bridge of his nose.
"Good news though. We will be sending it over to you free of charge of course, to any address within the United States."
Furcifer sighed. "Sure. Sure. But I want it back before the end of the day. And I'm in the UK." At the very least he wanted some expedited shipping out of this disaster. He checked his watch.

"Okay... I'll see what I can do."
"No, you will do it. I've been waiting two years for you to find that bag. Do you know how much Buzzfeed would enjoy this story? 'Man waits two years for lost luggage, Beta Airlines'

outraged response will stun you!'"
The lady audibly gulped. "Of course sir. Can I take down the address?"
Furcifer gave them their London address.
"Thank you sir." She said with her Southern swirl. "You have a nice day."
"Same, same." He hung up as she tried to give him a number to track the luggage with.

Furcifer sighed and put his phone away. "They found my luggage from Bangkok." He sighed.
Gabrielle raised an eyebrow. "What's in there?"
"Books, mostly. Notebooks and that kind of stuff." He sighed and sat back. "I'm really not sure I still need any of it but I'll be going through it regardless."
"Alright." Gabrielle hung the dishtowel back and peeked outside.
"The IMG hasn't posted any updates. Maybe they're giving up?" Shrugged Furcifer.
"They won't. They'll just try another approach, and that

worries me." Gabrielle turned away.

"It's alright." Furcifer looked over. "It's unlikely Twitch is going to press charges. Their lawyers have not made a move and ours have been busy."

She sighed. "I'm not worried about that part."

"There's no way they can get the spell." Furcifer tried to reassure her.

"I hope so, Furcifer. I hope so."

Chapter 26

S

The high street's frantic pace had slowed down, a good sign for Salem to close the small store. It was no good to spend too long in the tiny space, and he still had a way to go.

Ethan had come to see him before the ball, and warned him the Guild knew about him. He'd been a member fifteen or so years ago, when Redford was in charge, and they'd approached him multiple times about rejoining. He had said no every time. He'd hoped moving to London until he could cross the Atlantic would have helped and it had, to some degree. Being away from the Brussels headquarters made him just hard enough to find that they didn't bother.

He locked up the stand and walked towards the tube. Granted, Twitch's presence had unnerved him a bit. When the man came to pick up the book he'd not yet known the Guild was involved as well. Had he known, he wasn't sure if he would have given the book up. Twitch had no idea what he was getting himself into again. It had been a surprise to see the man, but a greater surprise the man did not seem to recognise him at all. At least he seemed to have changed for the better.

He tapped his Oyster card onto the card reader and walked through the gates and into the tube system. It was comforting - in a city this big he was just a random stranger. Nobody bothered him. And pretty soon he would have enough money to move away - maybe Alaska. His daydreams of lonely life were disturbed when he felt someone come up behind him. Immediately worried for pickpockets, he took hold of his bag and glared around. Nobody seemed to be going through his backpack. He sighed and boarded the first train coming, getting off at his stop.

Maybe he was just being paranoid, he thought to himself, as he got out of the tube station. Here, surrounded by greens and empty space, it was hard to think about danger. He rolled his head in his neck and yawned. It was only a ten minute walk home through the park, a little longer if he stopped by the grocery store to pick up dinner. His thoughts were drifting to what to make himself. Meatballs sounded great, he had a day off tomorrow and he'd be able to finish off any leftovers. He smiled at the thought and walked up to the park, almost not noticing someone was following him.

The sound of footsteps behind him put him on edge again. Perhaps he'd been a bit too fast in hoping nobody had followed him. He glanced aorund and dove into the park, taking the long road around the little church at the centre. He paused, hoping whoever was there would just walk on.

It was going to go dark soon - the park would be closed at twilight, so in about thirty minutes. He could wait it out till then, if need be, before leaving. At that point a police officer would do a quick round before locking up, and he could easily follow the cop out.

This was ridiculous. He rubbed his face, wondering if he really would be waiting for thirty minutes just in case some other pedestrian, who probably lived in the same area, wanted to rob him. The gravel around him was silent - barely a sound.

After listening to the quiet for a moment, he emerged from behind the church and looked around. Nothing suspicious - a mother pushing a pram was just leaving the park and turning towards the tube station. Salem sighed and hurried towards the north gate of the park. Just before reaching the gate, however, he felt a sharp pain in his neck. Someone behind him was throwing a punch and had hit him in the back of the neck. He gasped and turned around, almost stunned by the pain. Two men - he recognised one as the one that had been chasing Twitch. Another knock and he was out cold.

☆ ☆ ☆

His wrists had rubbed sore against the handcuffs and his back was aching from sitting bent over on the hard chair.
"This is no way to treat your elders, son."
Ramsey walked over. "If those elders were to tell me what I needed to know I would respect them." He said, crouching down before him.
"We have one of the books, the other has vanished. You had one at your stall. Where are the others?"
"I've told you before. No clue." He looked up. "Just downloaded it from some torrenting site, mate. Thought it was the new thriller by that famous author, you know, who wrote the book the movie with what's his name."
"You are testing my patience." Ramsey got up.

"And you mine, honestly. Who're the lackeys?" He nodded to some young mages, no doubt selected for their strong stomachs.

"Never you mind." He pulled the man's hair. "I need to know where the other books are. Ethan has gone awol, you sell one of the books, and suddenly Furcifer is running around making trouble."

"Isn't that what he usually does?" He raised an eyebrow.

"Just tell me the location. One book, and I let you go."

"No. Why do you even need to know?"

Ramsey looked over. "Redford needs to know."

He raised an eyebrow. "Really now? The icicle supreme has a need for things?"

"I'm not playing with you." He hissed.

"I'm not either. Let me go now and I'll be out of your hair." Salem tried a smile, but it opened up his cracked lip and sent some fresh blood flowing. The copper taste was awful.

"I'm done with this." Ramsey got out a knife, and the youths in the background shied away a little. Maybe their stomachs weren't too strong.

Salem closed his eyes and slowed his breathing. Some of the potion he'd used earlier to impress Furcifer had spilled onto his fingertips and under his fingernails, and he was rubbing it onto the handcuffs now. Hopefully it would be enough.

"Kid, what's your name?" He looked to one of the young ones in the background.

"Rebecca, sir." Rebecca cleared her throat. "I'm uh, not a fan of spiders."

The youth next to her made a face at that strange utterance.

"You might want to duck, Rebecca." Smirked Salem, before uttering the spell. The handcuffs turned pure gold, and he tore them open easily. He got up and grabbed Ramsey's wrist, pushing the dagger away, fingers closing around his wrist. Ramsey had been caught off guard and tried to struggle, but the other had a firm grip. Salem hooked his leg and kicked, unbalancing Ramsey enough to grab the knife. He winced - his first grab had caught the blade, but he now had the hilt. Ramsey fell to the ground but rolled away from Salem and got to his feet quickly, but Salem had the knife now. Ramsey tried to get behind him but it was no use - the other was getting close to him and lunged.

Ramsey again dodged narrowly, but he didn't manage to get any punches in. The man looked infuriated and crouched low, aiming to punch Salem in the stomach. This time Salem was dodging, but badly. He was stiff from hours on the chair. The hit connected and knocked the wind out of him.

A victorious Ramsey closed in and pushed him towards the wall, apparently planning to corner him. Salem still had a hold of the knife and this time used it, swinging at the man's face. Immediately, Ramsey backed away. One of the youths rushed up to try and help but Salem threw him back with a spell.

"This isn't your fight, kid." They would not be involved if he could help it. After all they were just mages trying to do what their leader demanded.

With that, the kid gasped and ran up the stairs, leaving the hatch open. Fresh air rushed in and Salem took a deep breath, almost forgetting about the fight. Ramsey shoved him and grabbed his wrist, but this time Salem got out of his grip and stabbed the man in the chest. The first stab barely made contact, deflecting off of a rib, but Ramsey was taken off guard. Salem took the opportunity and tried again, again stabbing the man. This time the knife slid in, and he was disgusted to hear the other man's gurgling breaths. He shoved the other away.

The fight was over.

“You know, by now Twitch will have the other book. I was hoping to keep you off of his tail for a bit longer, but if you start playing with knives...” He looked up. “Rebecca, right?”

Rebecca nodded, frozen stiff at the back. In the light that rushed in from the hatch he could tell she was about twenty, the uneven skin of puberty left behind but no real experience in her eyes.

“Sir....” She looked about ready to run. “We should get him help.”

“You’re with Ethan?”

The girl sighed relieved. “Yes sir. He asked me to try and stay close to Ramsey. And that you would know if I said that I was afraid of spiders. I'm not.”

Salem nodded. “I do. That's how I knew you were on his

side."
"Well, that assignment is over. Get me out of here and bring me up to date."
Rebecca nodded. "I uh... But we can't leave him here...."
What an inconvenience. Salem shook his head. "We'll call an ambulance when we're up top. Don't worry."
Rebecca shivered and grabbed the keys from Ramsey before leading the way up the stairs.
"Ethan's in the UK, sir. He was sent to a fundraising thing, I think so they could search his room and keep him away from the search." Rebecca explained.
Salem nodded. "I know. He came to see me." He said. Ethan would have brought the book along to bring to Twitch. Which raised another question.

"Does the IMG know where Twitch is?"
"No. Not last I heard." Rebecca said, looking over. "They uh, don't really know what he looks like, either."
"That'll work in our favour, it seems." He walked up the stairs with the boy and groaned.
"Let me help you." Rebecca rushed to support the mage. Somewhere in the fight Ramsey had gotten a slash in - he felt the skin on his side pull painfully as he stretched out. He leaned onto the young lady.
"Can you contact Ethan?"
"I can try." Rebecca said. She only knew bits and pieces about

the operation – Ethan had thought that to be the safest.
"Alright then." He took a deep breath and walked up the stairs, taking a breath of fresh air as they left what seemed to be a basement.
Rebecca set him down on a kitchen chair. "The house is rented, I don't know for how long. It's in Ramsey's name."
"That's fine. Nothing of this will lead to you." Salem looked over at her. "If you leave your phone, you could just walk out. I won't hold it against you." He gave the young woman a grave look.
Rebecca bit her lip but then shook his head. "No. I'm here for this. Ethan told me it could get hairy."
"You have no idea. Where are we anyway?"
"Uh. It was a long way on an overground train. So... I think... " She sat down. In all the excitement it seemed she had paid very little attention.
"Station names?"
"Woking. We got off at Woking and we rented a car." She nodded. "Then we drove into London to... get you."
Salem took off his top with a groan. "First aid kit." He looked up.
"What? Oh!" Rebecca shot up and rushed around to try and find the kit. "Is it bad?"
"Stings. But it'll be fine. Just a bad graze." He said. He hoped he could get away without stitches at this point.

Rebecca winced at the wound. "Ouch." She said, putting the first aid kit down next to the man.
Salem took in a deep breath and looked over. "It'll be fine." He said, opening the box with one hand and grabbing the disinfecting spray.
"You, call Ethan." He said as he sprayed the wound. It looked like the other kid had ran - he hoped he was okay. The nearest headquarters for the Guild were a country over and there would not be much support for this kind of undercover operation.

Rebecca swallowed and nodded, grabbing the phone. It was clear she wanted to get out of here, and with some luck, Salem could send her home soon. The disinfectant stung, but that was the least of his worries right now.

Chapter 27

It had taken Twitch some time to open the letter. When Ethan gave it to him in the sewers it had not been the time or the place, but now he had no reason to put it off any further. Shaky fingers tore open the envelope and pulled out the yellowed paper.

My Dearest Redford,

I hope this letter finds you in the best of health. I am afraid I have bad news.

Remember how, in a far away past, we would chuckle at the accounts of young Victorian girls fainting at the merest display of magic, whether it was a trick or reality? I feel myself much like one of them now, overcome and impressed by a magic I do not understand, but hopefully, some day someone will mock me knowing exactly what has caused the phenomenon I have seen and dismiss my fear as a childish reaction to an unknown power.

What led us to this spell was the old question. How much of our magic knowledge has been lost over the years? How much did our ancestors know about magic, pure magic, not the folklore. What did the ones known as witches and wizards know? There is only one way to reach far enough back to find the answer to this question, and that is to cross the boundaries of time and life itself.

You warned us against proceeding with the Ritual we had prepared, but I must admit it has not deterred us. In fact, a few of us, Lyra and Adison, saw your dismissal of the Ritual as a challenge and doubled our efforts. You proposed that the mere quantity of potions and herbs required would prove insurmountable, but over the last months we have gathered enough to lay out the circle for the spell. Granted, we have had to grow some of the herbs ourselves, which was difficult at best, painstaking at worst. The roots of the plant you thought extinct we found in a strange little Chinese tea warehouse, and we recovered enough of it that with tender care and frequent watering, it sprang a fresh plant and planted new roots into its carefully selected soil.

Oh Redford. If I knew then what I knew now... I would have stopped all of this in its tracks. I would have smashed the plant pots and potion containers. But it is useless to dwell. All I can do now is provide you with a reliable account of the proceedings and hope that you can warn others against trying it. I have torn up the spell and hidden phrases in several spellbooks. Any ambitious mage would have to locate all seven spell books, find the specific phrase and then reconstruct it into the correct order. None of us will ever give any clue as to the spell's phrasing.

We set the Ritual in motion at eleven in the evening. The seven of us made our way to the warehouse in small groups. I came with Adison. Lyra, Regina and Estelle walked there from Regina's house. Vicky and Cassandra arrived last. We drew the figures on the floor and placed down the herbs and concoctions. As we burned the herbs, the smell grew... indescribable. Sweet and meaty, like the smell of death. This would prove to be rather ironic, later on. Estelle was clearly uncomfortable with it and remained mostly to the side, relighting herbs where necessary.

We started by praying. I know. You do not believe in the one God, but we did, and what we were about to do was so blasphemous we felt we lost some of our humanity as we begged Him for forgiveness. I remember Lyra cried. When we had gathered ourselves enough to start, we chanted the first part of the spell. It is meant to open the gates from where the spirit should return from. As the sound died away, Lyra and me brought out the body. This had been the most difficult item to obtain. A person, burned as a witch, with enough of their remains intact to be revived. It had been a long quest to find such a tomb, but we found it, in the communal tomb of a family by the name of Ward. Eight children, seven girls and one son, of which only one was burned as a witch. The others quietly lived out the rest of their lives, moving closer into the village and avoiding anything that could bring suspicion to themselves. They had obviously no desire to end up at a stake themselves.

Once the body had been lowered into the circle, the restoration part of the spell commenced. This would bring shape back to the body, enough to hold a spirit. The research we did specified this spell was not necessary to receive information, but to bring a spirit back to its own decayed husk... That seemed unnecessarily cruel to us. We were well aware we would only get one attempt to do this, we could not risk the spirit decaying because it had no flesh body to attach itself to. As we chanted, the body regained its shape, regrowing skin and muscle.

Imagine our surprise when the one we had picked to be our witch turned out to be a wizard! The history books had been vague, specifying only an A. Ward had been burned at the stake. We had expected it to be one of the daughters, Anabelle or Alice.

It turned out to be Asa, the youngest boy of the household. At this point we debated halting the ritual. In restoring the body we had already discovered lost lore, and we all agreed that it was this third part of the spell that was truly monstrous. Our souls would be lost for playing with such magic. I must admit quavering for a moment, but Estelle grabbed my hand and nodded for me to continue. We still could have closed the gates we had had opened and left, but I pressed on.

I must admit I took up the mantle of leader on this. The girls needed a strong figure and I was the eldest, the bravest. I was closer to my thirties than any of them and had studied the most magic. I nodded at Estelle and started the chant.

That last chant, Redford! It is less the sound of magic and more like the sound of forgotten gods. It has a lack of vowels no spell should have, and the words are mangled and hideous as we called to powers we did not understand at that point.

Perhaps it was our imagination, but the earth shook as we chanted. The portal we had opened suddenly became visible and there was a great howling! It was hair raising We had opened a door to let one out, but many sprang out, leaping to freedom.

I fear that this was what caused the death count. I could see one of the spirits try to enter Lyra, but she convulsed and fell dead. Three more of us suffered a same fate before we found a protective spell to ward them off and managed to find the one soul we needed.

At this point, there was only Adison, Cassandra and I left. Had we needed any more chants, we would not have lived. As soon as the soul we required was lead to the body, we closed the portal. Any soul which found itself out, without a body to cling to, evaporated with a shrill noise.

And then it was silent. I remember Cassandra's sobs as she tried to rouse Estelle and Lyra. Adison was still guarded, muttering protection spells to herself and looking around. I walked over to the body. He looked... alive. His chest was drawing in breath and his face was flushing, as if he was experiencing a bad dream. Within minutes he sat up with a cry which made me wince. It was nothing like the cries from the souls we had heard, but it carried the same pain and anguish.

Cassandra gasped and approached him, holding a hand out. He ignored it and sat up, demanding a covering of some sort, before noticing his surroundings and screaming once more. He demanded to know who had done this. It was hard for me to confess that I had done this, but you know me, Redford. I bowed my head and admitted to being the one.

He hated me for it. He was fearful and angry at the same time, distrusting of us until we demonstrated we had powers like him.

We have sent him to a hospital to regain his power, but I fear we have done the wrongest thing. He is hateful, distrusting and despises humans. The hospital has often called me, saying he has mistreated a nurse. Only my pleading with them has kept him from being turned away.

When he is strong enough I will induct him into the Scribes. A strong magic based community, away from humans, should prove beneficial for him. He has also taken a liking to my young son Ethan.

I'm afraid this is the end of that story. The Spell is hidden away and cannot do any more harm. It was at best a rudimentary, badly written spell but you cannot deny its efficiency. In fact I encourage you to come meet Asa. He prefers to be called Twitch, and he is a good conversational partner. His ideas about magic are quite interesting.

Yours always,

Henrietta Finch

Chapter 28

Twitch yawned a little as he packed up his stuff to head home. It had been a long day at the school and he was happy it was over - he had quite a few quizzes to correct. He'd tested the older kids to see what they had remembered from the classes before his absence but they had struggled. This job really was more demanding than he had thought it could ever be. Not to mention he would have to do a pop quiz on Napoleon at some point. He gathered up the papers and tucked them in his drawer before leaving the classroom. Tomorrow he only taught for a few hours, he could leave the grading until then. Right now he just wanted to get home and crash into bed. It had been a hectic week, and he was still working on decrypting the hints Henrietta had given him. With Ethan joining him he now had three books, and a pretty good idea of where the fourth was. With a sigh he took out his phone and texted Furcifer.

I got three books. I don't know what to do to get the fourth yet, though. May need help. Ethan's at my house. Don't go there.

He sighed. Really he just wanted to avoid the mage trying to steal the books from him and going after them on his own.

The only issue was he could not get all of the books on his own. Reaching out for help was... painful. They... Gabrielle had caused him so much pain. For months he had been unable to sleep soundly.

Before he put the phone away, he fired off another text, this one to Salem.

Hey, don't know what you've been up to. Please let me know if you have any more info on the books. I could really use your help on this. This is Twitch, by the way

This one was really a shot in the dark. Salem could just as easily say no, but there was something there, something he thought he could count on.

Deep in thought, he left the classroom.

Lydia bumped into him. “Hey! What’s on your mind, you look pensive.”
“Oh! Thinking about dinner, really.” He lied quickly. “How about you, you’re here late.”
“Ah, I always grade tests the same day.” She said, stretching out. “How about dinner together? There’s a decent pub on the corner.”
“Sure.” Nodded Twitch, before realising he had other things to do. Then again... He did not want to back out of this. She had asked and he had said yes. And it was not like she’d had to twist his arm. It even surprised him how fast he’d said yes.

“Wonderful! They do a great roast chicken.” She said, patting his shoulder.
“Sounds great. So how’s it working out with the spellbook?”
“Pretty great.” She had to admit, looking down at her hands. “I’ve been working on the basic spells. You know, the ones that just do the one simple thing. Finding spells work really well for me for some reason so that makes me happy. I found like sixteen bobby pins and three library cards just with an afternoon of practice.”
He laughed a little, enjoying the sparkle in her eye.
“That’s great! To get so good at that fast is really, really impressive.” He felt a warmth inside him as he looked over to her.

"Seems like you have found your speciality then." He nodded.
"You can have specialties?" She looked over. "I thought it was all learning and practice."
"It is. To some degree." He shrugged. "But you can be good at a specific kind of spell through innate talent." He smiled over a bit.
She took a deep breath. "Looks like I'm good at finding stuff then. So, let's go find this pub, It's called the Prince William." She grinned. "You probably know all about it." She teased.
"Oh don't get me started. There's plenty of famous Williams in history. William of Orange, Rory Williams..."
She lightly swatted him and laughed. "That last one's not real."
"Oh he was, he was a famous centurion."
She shook her head. "You're terrible." She said, walking out of the school with him and heading down the road. It was getting chilly as the sun set.
"So how did your day go?" Twitch asked.
"Pleasant enough." Lydia answered. "The kids weren't too

much of a nightmare."
"They must have been tired out after my class." He looked around and nodded at a sign hanging out at the end of the road, near the corner.
"That the pub?" They were really not far off, but it was hard to be far away from a pub at any time in this city. It had only taken them a few minutes to get there.
"Yep!" She said and opened the door for him.

Ah, the usual smell of beer and food.
Twitch smiled and looked around. "Great choice of place."
It was a warm looking place with nice wood and red cushioned seats. People chattering over a tv playing some football. Very old fashioned. Very what he needed right now. Warm and crowded. It was wonderful - it felt like a large lounge and the presence of people made him feel more normal.

Despite his bravado about getting the notebooks, he was terrified. Anything that could steer him away, he would follow... Soon, however, he needed to do this. If he did not the notebooks would all be found and not by him, but by people who would use this for the wrong purposes.
"Penny for your thoughts?"
"Huh?" Twitch blinked and looked over.
"It's - nevermind. What are you thinking about?" The warm lights of the pub illuminated her curls and coral lips.

"Oh, just a chore I have later." He tried to play it off.

"Sounds boring." She grabbed a seat in one of the quieter parts of the pub and picked up the menu.

"I guess I am." He chuckled and followed her lead. "So the chicken huh?"

"Yup. I'm half convinced they put crack in it." She replied, glancing over the menu. "Ah, I can pretend but I'm getting the chicken burger anyway." She laid the menu down and shook her head.

"Same for me then. I trust your recommendation. And uh... A milkshake."

"You are so American!" She laughed, though she had never figured out his ethnicity. His accent definitely wasn't local.

"I am not. I actually am English... I just lived in Zeus City for a long time." He smiled and looked over.

"Really? I would not have believed you. Why did you move back?"

"Well... I had an issue with my landlady." He shrugged. It wasn't really a lie. Technically, Gabrielle had been his landlady. And they definitely had issues.

"Ah... So you basically move all the way out here?"

"Well... Yes. I don't like half assing my good byes." He looked up a little and smiled.

"That you don't." She looked around. "I don't think they have milkshakes, though."

The meal tasted wonderfully, Twitch had to admit, and they were talking the whole meal through.
“That was wonderful.” He said, opening the door for her. The bill hadn’t been too bad either, for a meal out.
“So you really are serious about doing this thing...” She took a deep breath. “Has it got to do with magic?”
He sighed, having hoped he could avoid speaking about it altogether.
“Yes, it does. Something happened in my past and... I want to help set it right.” He looked over.
“Okay.” She seemed to hesitate. “Can I help? I’m magic now.”
“Don’t take this the wrong way, but you’re very new at magic. And technically you were magic all along.” He looked over to her. “At least to me.”
She smiled a little and took his hand, giving it a little kiss.
“I feel the same way.”
Twitch blushed and took his hand back. “Ah, really?”
“Mmm.”
“I -” He swallowed. “I don’t know what to say.”
“Which is why you should let me come.” She smiled. “Come on. Let me help you out.”
He groaned. “I... It’s a long story.”
“Then tell me.” She took his arm and smiled. “We’ve got a long walk to my apartment ahead.”
And so he started telling her everything.

Chapter 29

Furcifer put the phone down and looked over to Gabrielle with a grin.

"Twitch has three books and he knows where the fourth is." It felt like a victory, already. They needed some good news after all this.

He looked out the window. The sun was setting and their tails had long wandered off. Furcifer was eager to get the last piece of the puzzle.

Gabrielle nodded slowly.

"What is it?" Furcifer looked over to her with a sigh. She was distracted, obviously worried.

"He still won't want me near there."

"That's very likely." Said Furcifer. "But I'll want you there. So... we'll find a way, okay?"

"So now he's got three books, we've got one, IMG has one.... And there's another two out there."

Furcifer nodded. "He knows where one of them is, he said. So we'll have the majority of books and they can't do anything

with just one book."
Gabrielle crossed her arms, silver curls bouncing. "Still." She said, picking up one of the notebooks and looking through it. "What if we're missing something?"
"We're not. You're worrying too much. The real danger was not in a single notebook being found randomly. It was in all of them being found together and the spell being used." He put his hand on her shoulder.

Gabrielle looked down at the notebook. Furcifer followed her gaze. For all their work they hadn't even found the first part of the Spell in the original notebook. They knew what they were looking for - so Furcifer doubted the IMG had made any progress either. Perhaps... The first part was not in the first book. What if it was in the last? That would make sense - Gabrielle would not want someone who found the books on accident realise it was part of The Spell. So once they found...

"Has anyone looked into Ethan yet?" Gabrielle asked.
"Huh?" Furcifer shook his head, annoyed at the interruption of his thoughts. "Of course we have. He's been in the IMG the last few years. There's no way he had anything to do with this. Even his mother said he hadn't visited in ages."
Furcifer nodded. "Twitch said he's with him... "
"You don't say? I don't trust it."
"Not surprised." Furcifer said blankly. The woman next to

him had a keen, if overly sharp mind.
"Look, he's with Twitch. We can stay away from them for as long as possible just in case he is an IMG spy." Furcifer said. They had kept their information pretty separate for the last little while anyway.
Gabrielle put down the notebook again. "So we're on our own with this one. Until Twitch gives us more."
"We've been on our own before. We're good at being on our own." Furcifer smirked. "Don't worry."

He looked up as the doorbell rang. "That must be my luggage at last!" He huffed and got up. After a few failed deliveries and attempts, he hoped they had gotten it right this time! He rushed to the door and opened up.

At least it looked promising. The courier was dragging a large, plastic wrapped shell style suitcase behind him. It looked somewhat battered, but still intact.
"Thank you!" He dragged the suitcase inside and slammed the door in the courier's face.
There was an insistent knocking. "Sir, I need your signature!"
"Come back in two years!"
Seeing Gabrielle glare, Furcifer groaned and opened the door to sign the man's pad. "There. Now scram!" He saw the man run off.

"Finally." He huffed, dragging the bag further inside and dropping it on the floor of the lounge to tear the plastic and open it up.

It was a strange reunion. Such old and familiar books, which he had thought were completely lost. Immediately the memories came back as he opened the bag.

"Huh... Oh! I completely forgot about this herbology book... Ooh I'm going to enjoy reading that one..." He paused as he took out another book.

It had a blue cover, in a very familiar style. One of the notebooks they had been hunting.

"Oh you have got to be kidding me." He paged through the book, looking up to beckon Gabrielle closer. "I uh, guess we just found another one of the notebooks..."

Gabrielle popped her head into the room. Seeing the scene she sighed.

"In your old lost luggage. You found one of the books, in your old, lost luggage?"

"I must have picked it up at a market or something... I am just glad it turned up." He nodded and paged through it.

"That must have been the one hidden at one of the temples. So I don't even want to know how you got it." She sighed and looked over. "Alright. Have ten minutes of fun with it. Then we need to get back to work. There is still a lot to do." She took out her phone and tapped something in. Most likely she was finishing some kind of to do list, where the book was merely an unchecked list item. Furcifer shook his head and sat down, happy with his new toy.

"Oh my gosh this has a spell to make slow brew coffee!"

"Isn't that basically cheating?" She peeked out from over her phone. "Sit still. I'm trying to take pictures of the book."

"What for?"

"Proof that we have it."

He sighed but held the book upright for her. She snapped a few pictures and tapped away on her phone.

"Want to try this magical cold brew?"

"Sure." She nodded and put the phone away to go grab some

glasses. "Go on."
Furcifer grinned and let her set the glasses down before reading the spell.
"All looks pretty decent." He said, licking his lips.
There was always that moment of nerves using a spell you hadn't created yourself. Furcifer generally didn't like it, but he wanted to enjoy the moment, this victory. Using this spell would be a good start. It made sense to him at least.

Gabrielle sat down at the table and looked over, an amused smile on her face.
"Okay. Here goes. It's a bit sloppy but..."
"It was probably written before you were even born, Furce. Just use it."
Furcifer made a face but then started uttering the spell. Some of the words caused him to stumble and he had to pause at a few points to see how to proceed. Finally, when it was done, he focussed on the glasses.
Nothing happened. The glasses were still empty, a little shiny in the reading lamp's light. It was getting too dark for the lamp alone but dusk had come so slowly he hadn't even thought to turn on the light.
"That's very strange." He said, reaching a hand out to the book.
It made a loud snapping sound and closed tight. Furcifer felt it graze his fingernails.

"Whoa!" He jumped up. Now the book was not just closed, there was a snarling sound coming from it.

The blue cover turned black and green, and Furcifer was horrified to see green slime ooze from the spine.

Gabrielle jumped up as well, grabbing the broom by the door.

Furcifer held a hand out. "No. Turn the light on!" He said, his curiosity getting the better of him.

"Furcifer. It's a trap mechanism of some kind!" She hissed, using the broomstick handle to flip the light switch.

"I know!" He looked over. "But it was dormant for over two years so I'm hoping it's still a bit slow." He approached it and tried to get a clear look at it.

"It's a monster." Gabrielle pulled the broomstick closer to her.

"No shit!" Furcifer dodged the creature spitting at him. The goop splat against the wall, and Furcifer could smell the plaster melting away. There was no question it would not be pleasant to get on his skin. He put up the hood of his hoodie and looked to Gabrielle.

"Stay behind it."

"Planning to!" She said, glaring over. "What, you think I'd let it get at me? It's going after you right now!"

"Thanks, Gabrielle. Knew you cared." He said, lunging

forward. The book anticipated him and snapped at his hand. It missed his hand by only a few centimeters.
"Alright... We need to get this to sleep again." He said. How did I get here, he wondered. This is some kind of rpg villain stuff. The thing snarled and shuffled around the table, sniffing the air. It emitted a low growl and turned towards the other end of the table, the acidic spit oozing from between the pages.

Gabrielle eyed the notes spread across the table, and he could guess what she was thinking. A book monster was unlikely to kill them, but it could eat any notes they had and harm them in the process. So far it seemed to be focussed on the paper.
With a sickening sound, it moved towards the paper, and Gabrielle's broom swept across the table, slamming the monster against the wall.
"Fuck!" Gabrielle said as it bounced and rushed up to her. The yellow teeth exposed, it opened up for a bite. Throwing over the table he ran over to teleport her away from it - it was going for the jugular.
Furcifer moved fast - he pulled her out of the thing's path. The thing crashed into his leg and seemed dazed. He gasped, momentarily dizzy with pain as it bit down. Thoughts of a bear trap entered his mind.

"Give me that." He took the broom from her and with measured precision, hit the monster towards the bathroom. The leather made a sickening squeak as it skidded across the tiles.

As soon as it had crossed the threshold to the bathroom, Gabrielle slammed her weight against the door to close it. There was a thumping from inside, but it couldn't get out.
"We need to kill that thing. And fast. I need to pee." Furcifer took a deep breath and tried to ignore the scary thumping from inside the bathroom. Now that the fight was over, or at least had paused, he felt the pain shoot up through his leg. If he looked at it now he would lose his resolve, but it felt like it had torn through some tissue when he had hit it.
"It bit you." Gabrielle hissed. "Shit. Sit!"
"We can't - it'll get out of that bathroom in a minute and then we'll be in real trouble." Furcifer said. "For now I can be of help. I've got about two more minutes before the pain hits fully and you'll be on your own." He was dizzy - pain and magic were not a good combination.

She looked over. "Alright. Looks like it might have been poisoned so stay awake until we can figure it out."
"Yes. Once we capture it or properly disable it we'll be able to make an antidote, or -"
"I didn't say talk."

"I'm trying to stay awake." He rolled his eyes. The thing banged on the door again and this time the hinges cracked.

"Alright." Gabrielle said. "I've got a plan. Go over there and open the door when I say so. Keep the door between yourself and the thing."

Furcifer jumped up. "Fine, but if you get bit too..."

"I'll be fine!" She glanced over. "Now do it!" She held the broom in both hands and moved her hands down the length of the broom. With one hand she gathered up the notes on the table and moved in front of it.

"Alright." He limped over to the door. His heart was pounding in his chest. Gabrielle, however, was no longer holding the broom as a weapon but more like a wand, pointing the shaft towards the monster. The smell of bile and blood filled the room.

"Ready?"

"I'm ready." She said, though he could sense the tension in her voice.

He nodded and ripped open the door, keeping the door between him and the thing. It shot forward, hesitated, then rushed towards Gabrielle once it realised it would stand in its way of getting at the papers.

Gabrielle barked out a spell and launched it at the book, but it was barely phased. The magic bounced off of it and hit the door behind it, leaving a large hole.

"Shit!" Gabrielle swept at the thing and kept it at bay. To Furcifer's horror, the mouth of the book thing opened up. The mouth enclosed the head of the broom and steadily moved upward. With a cry, Gabrielle shook the broom in an effort to dislodge it, but to no avail. Its teeth only bit deeper into the wood, producing loud cracking noises.

"Portal!" Gabrielle called out. "Best we can do is drop this thing through a portal somewhere. I hear the Mariana trench is nice this time of year."

He grimaced and tried to focus. Every time he tried to conjure up a magic spell, his head started swimming.

Gabrielle peeked over, noticing the issue he had. "It's okay. Shoddy spell will work for this." She reassured. "Just... focus on somewhere that is not crowded. Somewhere deserted... Maybe where it came from."

He nodded and looked over.

"Alright. I can do that." He focussed on a dense forest. His hiking holiday in Germany, last year. The smells of pines came through as he focussed and the bird song - a bird chirped in his ear.

A stream. It was right near him, and it mixed the scents into a clear, crisp mixture of fresh air.

He opened his eyes again and fired the portal spell. The portal opened up, a whirling vortex of purple until he finally settled the spell's magic. It was open enough that he could smell the forest now - and for a second he just wanted to step through himself.

"Get it through!" Gabrielle finally said, rushing to grab the broom and shove the thing through the portal.

"Ah!" Furcifer gasped and threw his weight forward to try and scare the thing into the portal. It was wobbling - the forest changed, now it was a bar he'd been in a while ago. And then a flash of a traffic light. A mountain cabin, which morphed into an office.

His grasp on the magic was loosening. He had to try and keep concentrated, though the pain was making him woozy and lose his focus.

He was becoming dizzy. The portal closing a little.

"Keep it up! You can do it!" Gabrielle pushed the book through, though it was biting down on her chainmail sleeve.

"Crap, crap!" She tried to pull loose, but its teeth were stuck in the mesh.

"The portal! I can't keep it open much longer." The diameter was shifting between one yard and half a yard. The book bit at her wrist but only managed to grab a beaded bracelet, which it swallowed right away.
She nodded, struggling to take off her top. Her movements were frantic as the portal closed, and she seemed to consider jumping through with it until she saw the location change once more.

Finally, with a big tug, she pulled the top and the layers under and over it over her head. The book tugged at the sleeve it had its teeth in and growled, acid like saliva dripping down. It tried to pull Gabrielle off balance. It seemed to be working. Furcifer could see her balancing on one leg. Again the scene behind the portal changed, and Furcifer tried to focus - that forest from earlier. He had to keep that one in mind.

Furcifer gasped. "Watch out!" He could not move- he had to focus on the portal. Gabrielle fell over, into the portal, dragging the book with her. The portal closed, and there was nothing left but a piece of bookmark.

Chapter 30

Gothball walked over Twitch's lap and settled into Lydia's, acting like he paid the rent in the house. Twitch absentmindedly stroked him. Ethan had left a few minutes after they got in - he'd told him it was to meet up with a friend, but he was half thinking the man just wanted to give him and Lydia some space to talk.

"I just... You are kidding aren't you?" She frowned, looking over. "Magic battles. Museum artefacts that brainwash. Spells that -"

"I know it's a tall order." He sighed and looked over. "But it's all true." He let Gothball swat at his hand and curled his fingers around the paw. It was easier to focus on the cat than on Lydia right now.

"Yeah but still. I mean. I did some magic research. I know what you told me about factions. But this is... Big, Asa."

He winced at the name. That seemed to be a bad sign, it put a distance between them. He finally looked up to her, hoping to see... He wasn't sure. Maybe acceptance?

Lydia lifted his head up a little. “Hey. I’m trusting you here okay?” She said, looking him in the eyes. “I mean, there’s a hospital out there where apparently a magic user is using magic to heal people.”

“That’s.... Kind of impossible. Magic can’t be used to heal, but it can be used to speed up the healing process, even so...”

“Twitch. I’m making a point.” She raised an eyebrow.

“Alright.” He said, looking over, smiling a little at the fact she was using his nickname again.

“So this spell is super important to them? To this guild?”

“I do believe they want to use it for something... And well, I don’t think it should be used.”

She nodded. “For reasons you’ve mentioned. Ohh. My head.” She put a hand to her forehead.

“Yeah... I guess it’s not everyday you find out...” Twitch smiled nervously. He had so much experience being alive and yet this was one of the hardest moments. First time he had really told anyway – first time he had told someone who did not have easy access to files on him. Someone he was invested in.

“Okay. So now you’re working on trying to find these books. Okay. And you fought a spider for one of them.”

He nodded solemnly.

“I could be helpful. I can locate things so very well you wouldn’t believe it.” She snapped her fingers. “Boom, found

my hairpin. Boom, found my coffee mug. It's -"
"You may just be a natural." He laughed. "It could be very helpful, I agree. I've texted another friend as well. But... I think there might not be many people I can ask for help on this."
Quickly, he checked his phone, remembering the text he'd sent to Salem.
There was a reply.

I'll help. Long story, but I've promised a friend. And I got one of their mages.

"Wow. Okay..." He said to himself and cleared his throat. "My friend uh, he might be up for this as well."
Hopefully, the meeting with Ethan would go well.
"Then it looks like you've got a team." Grinned Lydia. "Hey Gothball, do you want to be a mage as well? No? Okay." She laughed and looked over, and Twitch knew what he had seen in her was correct. She was kind, smart and wonderful. Hopefully after this there was still time for the both of them to become something.
"You're staring." She said softly, her hand pausing on Gothball's fur.

"Oh. I'm sorry. I was just..."
She grinned and sat up a little straighter, leaning in to kiss his lips. His heart was racing.
"No need to explain." She said. Her eyes moved over his face and he couldn't help it. When she kissed him, he closed his eyes and leaned in.
"Is your brother going to be gone for long?" She cleared her throat and opened her eyes.

Chapter 31

Gabrielle pulled off her tops, trying to get rid of the monster sinking its teeth into her nice chainmail top. Furcifer was telling something at her but it was hard to focus this close to a portal. There was a sound of wind rushing, which then changed to a forest like scene. The tug of the monster caught her off guard - she fell into the portal with a gasp. Oh no. And the damn thing was falling with her.

She hit the ground and rolled. It was not pleasant to fall into the mud and twigs. She sat up and gasped. The air was clean and crisp - not a trace of human civilisation. There probably wasn’t a road for miles around, not to mention the lack of any human structures. It looked virtually untouched.

Well how about that. She looked around and quickly grabbed her top, slipping it on. At the very least it offered some protection if the thing lunged again.

It was quiet. No trace of the monster, so far. There was a rustle that put her on edge, but it was a fox rushing into the bushes. Great. She landed in the one place that didn't have coffee. Or mobile coverage. She checked her phone and sighed. Damn. She straightened out her top and looked around.

At least it was a forest - that worked well enough. There was a stream nearby and she'd missed some rocks by inches. Where was the book, though? She had to secure it to avoid any hikers being injured by it or worse. After that she had to figure out how to get out of here. The book had eaten her bracelet with the commuter beads on it.

She got up and shivered. The sun was lowering in the sky and shadows were getting longer. It would get cold, fast. She rubbed her arms and started walking, making sure she headed in the same direction to not get lost.

Long ago, while engaged to Furcifer, she had organised her bachelorette party around a survival course. Needless to say she had enjoyed it more than her friends, but it was useful now. She knew to keep going in one direction and not to get turned around.

Five steps into her journey, she heard a whining sound.

"Oh. There you are." She said, spotting the book, cowering. Well. She couldn't leave it here, right? She crouched down.

“You’re getting cold huh?” She sighed and looked over. “Come on. We’re leaving this joint.”
The book grumped but then made its way over, jumping into her arms and burping out a bracelet.
“Ah, that’s where that went. Thanks.” She said tiredly and checked the beads. “Ah! Zeus City... Aiden.” She groaned and looked over. This meant she would have to deal with Aiden, something she had avoided for a while.

It was easier to pretend he didn’t exist, really. He didn’t fit into any way into her worldview - he was not part of a faction but he was a magic user. Last time they walked into each other was at a party and it had become awkward fast. And now she was going to have to call on his help.

“Okay... Here goes nothing.” She took one of the beads off of the bracelet and broke it on a stone. As the portal sucked them in, she hung onto the book.

Chapter 32

This time, Gabrielle relaxed as she went through the portal, which saved her more bruises on the other end. When she arrived though, she rushed to the bathroom and immediately threw up.

Russell looked up from his book as she teleported into the living room. He sighed.

"Excuse you. You didn't even chime and how did you get through the wards? This is our home you know." He got up and walked towards the bathroom.

"Commuter bead. Aiden made these." She held up what was left of her bracelet then threw up again. "Also wards only protect from portals in." She groaned and looked around.

"Where is Aiden?" She gulped, wiping her mouth.

"Hello to you too. Is that a Mimic Monster?" He pointed at the book on the floor, which was now biting on the couch.

"I guess so." She glanced around. There was just no time to be explaining herself to a non mage.

"Alright." Russell put the book he was reading away carefully.

Seemed he wanted to finish the book before it was eaten by a magical creature.

"Keep it away from Oni. We just got her to give up the tiny gremlin she found in the supermarket the other day."

"She's - Nevermind. You should let her play more. Especially with actual things that have magic." She shrugged and sighed. It was nice to warm up again after the brief wander in the cold.

"Yeah, and we also have to find someone to fix the TV. Aiden?" He peeked into the kitchen.

Aiden wiped his hands and came out. "Hi Gabrielle. I see you've been holding onto that commuter bead."

"Every time you owed me a favour you've given me one." She said.

"Hence why you only have one." Aiden added and put the towel down.

"Let's have tea. Furcifer tried calling me a few times. Is this about the trouble with the IMG? Also is that a mimic?"

"Kind of. It's asleep, ok?" She looked over. It seemed the thing had entered a state of rest

"We uh, Twitch at least, is looking for the books of the Spell. And... I can use your help. Please." It felt kind of weird to have to ask. But at this moment she needed help, even just to get back to the Elite headquarters.

Aiden sighed. "What do you need?" He asked.

She let out a breath she had been holding. "Thank you."

“Hold on.” Russell frowned. “Why are we helping her?
Gabrielle groaned. “I get it. You don't like me.”
“That's not it. I thought we were meant to be neutral?” He licked his lips and Aiden nodded.
“I do agree.” He said. “If we help you, you are the ones who... well. There's a war on out there.”
Gabrielle sighed exasperatedly. “I am asking for a ride back to my home. Not your undying loyalty and my name tattooed on your ass.”
“Language!” Russell huffed.
Gabrielle held her hands up. “Alright, alright. I get it. I'm the evil crone. But I really could use your help. If we – these books. We need to get rid of them.”
Aiden sighed. “I do get that, but he's got a point. I am neutral ground in this city.”
“We would need you in the United Kingdom, Aiden. Nobody here will find out and you'll be on the right side of this.”
“Really? Were you on the right side?” Aiden asked.
Gabrielle winced. She was losing him here. “I – I did stupid stuff.” She admitted.
“Help me set things right. I probably am not going to go back to the UK but Furcifer and Twitch will need help.”
“I'll consider it.” Aiden bit his lip. “So uh, you're taking the book right?”

"Yes. Yes!" She nodded and went to pick up the book - at least at the headquarters they would be able to deactivate it.
"I hope this time nobody dies." Russell said wryly.
"Seriously? I did not kill your friend!" She said, jumping up.
"You did a lot of other nasty things."
"Maybe but... "
"And now maybe my boyfriend won't come home."

"I've just about had enough of you!" Gabrielle turned around and launched a spell at Russell, who turned into a frog.
Gabrielle blinked. "Oh. Oh my word. I am so so sorry it's-" She really felt her frayed nerves right now. "I guess I'll get a taxi. After I turn your boyriend back."
"I'll get it." Aiden raised his hands. "You, get out. I'm done. Call me tomorrow and maybe I'll be in a better mood." He chased her out and picked up Russell.

Chapter 33

Ethan took a deep breath as he walked up to the bar, reading the unfamiliar names on the taps. The smell of beer was kind of stale, and he could not forget this was not familiar ground. The low light and multitude of people around didn't help. There was very little magic in the air, so he could rest assured. He moved with purpose and looked around for the man he was to meet here - a mage by the name of Salem.

He had known Salem for a while but more from his file than anything else. The IMG had files on everyone magically active whom they thought might be an asset. As they only did a recruitment drive every few years, they kept lists of people to invite just to make sure that every time, their slots would be filled. It was a thing of pride for them at this point. Salem had left a while ago, but they kept trying to find him to invite him back.

Whether he would ever rejoin was another thing - from what he had seen, he doubted the man would join any faction. And that was dangerous to factions. They didn't like mages who thought they could make it on their own.
The magic scene was splitting up and anyone in the middle between factions could be seen as a spy once a real war broke out. Neutrality was the enemy of factions, especially for the IMG with classified files everywhere.

And that was part of Ethan's plan. Releasing files only the IMG had access to would diminish their appeal and destroy their reputation for most people. It was not just keeping track of mages, either, but also offshore accounts and embezzlement. Considering how much they had been lobbying for government funds from Zeus City, Ethan knew the bombshell would land well with mages and non-mages alike. Even their generous contributions to mage issues could not help them there.

Of course, the reason he was thinking of their recruitment practices in the first place was because it was likely the IMG had approached Salem first. Of course the whole kidnapping could have been faked - so that Ethan would believe him. By now the IMG would know about his desertion. There were so many layers of leadership in the IMG that even with his connections, he would never see a plot to take him down coming. With this crowd he had to learn to expect anything.

He blinked and focused back on the area in front of the bar. His eyes darted around, mapping the place. One large entrance, one fire exit and stairs down to the bathroom. Behind the bar was a door to the kitchen, but one would have to jump over the bar. The stairs down to the bathroom were carpeted, but with a bend at a plateau, where a sofa was set to make the place look more luxurious. An obstacle which would make a turn much steeper if you had to run down.
He looked back to the entrance.

Of course, there was always the possibility that Salem was not coming and that he was too paranoid. But why risk it? Best to be prepared for the worst. He touched a commuter bead, which he had obtained at great cost, in his pocket.

From the corner of his eyes he saw the tall sullen man come in through the front entrance, immediately closing it behind him.

Ethan raised his hand then turned to the bar.

"Wasn't sure you were going to show." He said softly.

"Same." Said Ethan. "A drink?"

"No. I don't expect this to be a very long meeting." He looked over the man. "Are you alone?"

"I am. I was hoping for a long meeting."

"Depends on what you want." Salem rubbed his red wrists.

"I'm sorry that happened to you." He nodded, and Salem immediately covered up.

"I've got Rebecca still." He said, in a warning tone. "I will use her against you."

"You won't need to. I'm here for the same goal you are. To help Twitch get rid of the Spell."

"You sure? You did join the IMG." Salem's eyes glanced around.

"I'm alone here." He reassured. "And now that I know what I know."

"Unfortunately you haven't quite earned my trust." He said and shook his head.

"I hope to. What if I took you to Twitch? Would that reassure you?"

"Says who you don't take me back to some underground

basement?" He hissed.
"You said you have Rebecca still. She can stay in touch and you can just tell her to call for help if you don't come back."
He ordered two glasses of water. There was no use sitting around looking suspicious without so much as a drink.
"Also who says Twitch is working with you and not just a prisoner like I was?"
"I don't know how I can reassure you about that. But you reached out to me. And Rebecca knows what I stand for." He said.
"Why are you betraying your faction?" He popped the question.
"Because..." He sighed and looked away. "Because it's rotten. It's been rotting for a long time now. Long before Quentin."
Salem sighed and sipped the glass of water, biding his time, it seemed.
"And what are you going to do about it?"
"I'm going to expose them.
Right now it seemed Salem trusted Rebecca more than he did him. Which made sense. The two of them had been in that basement, witnessing some very hard things.

"Alright. But I want the first meeting to be on my terms. Neutral terrain. Rebecca comes along." He said.
"I can do that." Nodded Ethan. "Just give me a time and place."
"Alright." Salem got up. "I'll meet you where the last book is hidden. Two days."
With that he got up and walked to the door, weaving through the crowd.
Ethan let out a breath. Damnit. The pressure was on now. Then again it had been on ever since he had stepped out of his room at the IMG. Perhaps even before that, when he started realising that maybe his faction had malevolent ideas.

Chapter 34

The phone rang, and Furcifer picked up before even checking the number. The safe house was still a mess - he had taken the hours since Gabrielle's disappearance to rest up and treat his own wounds.

"Gabrielle?" He took a deep breath.

It was another voice, deeper.

"No... It's Aiden." He said softly. "I uh, Gabrielle swung by. I saw her off to the headquarters." He said.

The man's tone was dark. Almost ominous. "You're not coming are you?"

"No." Aiden said. "I can't be a part of this. If you need me to send you supplies, I can do that. But I won't make the trip for your wild goose chase."

Furcifer closed his eyes. So far, he'd always been able to count on his friends. Even Twitch and Russell were somewhat nice to him, or at least polite. His mind raced as he tried to figure out just what this meant for their search.

"You're not coming." He repeated.

"No." Said Aiden. "I would say I'm sorry but Gabrielle turned my boyfriend into a toad."
"No need to ribb-it in." Furcifer tried to joke. Aiden merely chuckled.
Furcifer tried to get angry. How dare Aiden - but it didn't happen. Instead there was a deep feeling of loneliness. Gabrielle wasn't even here to tolerate him.
"Alright. Thanks for letting me know. Give my best to Russell and Persephone." He could hear Aiden hesitate, probably surprised he knew Oni's full name.
He hung up and sat back, closing his eyes. The main reason he wanted Aiden here was to have at least someone who would be on his side.

They would be doing this the way Twitch wanted, it seemed. He picked up his phone again and texted Twitch.

`Truce. Gabrielle is back in the US.`

An answer came a few minutes later.

`Alright. I would be happy for your help. We're going after the last book.`

`Where is it?`

`Can't just tell you over phone. Meet up and we'll plan.`

Furcifer sighed at that, but he realised the man was right. They were dealing with some people who did not care for their privacy or safety. He shook his head and packed up everything in the safe house, so it could be shipped back to the US. He did not think he would be coming back here.

At the very least, he was back in the game.

Chapter 35

Rebecca smiled at the texts she had received. The youth had spent most of her morning on her mobile.

Ethan threw his hands up briefly. "Can you believe it?" He shook his head. "That girl just keeps texting like her life depends on it."

Twitch chuckled. "You were the same at that age. Remember Margaret?"

Ethan raised an eyebrow. "Oh gosh. You know she married a realtor in the end? That guy named Edward she went to prom with."

"No way." He snorted and looked over. It was silent for a moment before Twitch looked up again.

"It's gonna be tight. I mean, I know just about where to look, but..." He shook his head.

"We need Salem on this." Ethan sat down by Twitch. "Maybe if you call in..."

"Furcifer?" Twitch sighed and looked over. "As much as I hate to admit it, I'm not sure he'll want to join. Besides, I don't think the Guild is in this race anymore and that was his main reason for joining."

He blinked as Furcifer sent him a message. "Speak of the devil. He does want to join." He replied to the other to come meet up. His house had become a sort of headquarters for this quest.

Ethan nodded. He had been quiet about his meeting with Salem, and he wondered why. What was going on in that head of his?

"So how was Salem?" He pressed a little.

"Oh, he was good. Pissed off about the IMG but that's the kind of fire we need."

"And he just trusted you?"

"He trusts Rebecca." He nodded to Rebecca, who was now hunting around for a phone charger. "But yeah. Rebecca is the one he likes the best."

Rebecca looked up, released from her smartphone from the time being, and shrugged.

"I guess I'm just the most charming one. Anyway, are you

guys working on where we need to go cause that's kind of important." She looked from Twitch to Ethan.

Twitch sighed. "I know, just about." He had to admit. "I mean, let me just study the text to make sure I get it completely right." There was no point in rushing this only to arrive at the wrong area. Best case, Salem would help them find it.

Worst case, the IMG found it before them.

It still amazed him that Salem would know the location of the last book. How could he know? He shook his head until Rebecca's voice broke through.

"Then what are we doing here? Come on. Faster this is over the faster I can go out with Manon." The youth raised an eyebrow.

"I guess you tore up your IMG membership card then, Romeo?" Ethan chuckled and glanced over.

Rebecca sighed. "I don't think there will be much of the IMG left after all this."

Twitch nodded slowly. It seemed they had staked their reputation on finding the Spell. The resources they spent alone would be enough to bankrupt them.

Ethan nodded. “Hey, not having a faction is a valid option.”

“But having one isn’t a horrible idea either.” Twitch interjected. Life was so much easier with a faction. There were always people present to bounce ideas off, to have dinner with when you were lonely. Without a faction life was hard. Or at least it seemed that way to him.

Up until recently he had been with the witch faction, until it had merged with the Hopefuls two years earlier. At that point he had left, but not just for that reason. So many things had converged to help him make that decision it had felt like fate.

Life on his own had not been easy and he was sort of hoping Ethan would stick around. But perhaps his fantasy of forming his own little coven with Ethan and Lydia was just that, a fantasy.

Rebecca smiled, as if she could see the rift in their opinions.

“It’s fine. I’ll figure it out.” She said, with all the confidence of youth. “Just tell me where you need me for this one and I’ll be there.”

Twitch nodded and walked to the kitchen to grab a snack. “I’ll have a location ready to go in a few hours.”

“I hope so. It looks like we won’t have all that much time.” She took a deep breath.

Twitch nodded. They would need to be there when Salem showed up if they wanted to have a chance.

Chapter 36

I wonder when this is going to be over. I'm so tired waiting around for people and they won't tell me much. Rebecca xx

Same tho. They're treating us like kids and it sucks! Manon

Wish u were here. I can’t wait to see u.

Same. T_T I miss u.

I lo

At that point, Rebecca stopped typing and sighed. It was too early for the L word. If she used it now that would maybe just scare her off. Instead, she backspaced on that and sent a few emoji of a monkey and a few kisses. Darn. She really did like her. Manon was energetic, smart, ambitious and fun to be around, always had well thought out opinions and was better at magic than she was. They'd met at a magic camp which wasn't too bothered about several factions' children being in the same location and they had just... to say it with a cliche, clicked.

Rebecca glanced around and put the phone away. Ethan and Twitch were nice, but she really wanted this to be over with. She was missing school for this, even if said school had made her an accomplice to a kidnapping. That thought still haunted her. What if the police found her? Would she go to jail? She shivered. She looked over to Twitch, asleep over his books, and Ethan who had dozed off on the couch. It was getting late and she seemed to be the only one with her stomach in knots over this.

`It's getting late. Goodnight princess`

She texted before putting the phone away. One by one, she turned off the lights, looking around.

"Hey." Twitch, whom she thought had been fast asleep, was rubbing his nose.

"Hey. It's bed time." Rebecca yawned demonstratively.

"I know, I know. I'm going in a second." He closed the book. "Thanks for getting the lights. I think we can leave Ethan on the couch."

Rebecca nodded, glad she had her sleeping bag. At least the house was warm with thick carpeting, which would make finding a spot to sleep easy.

"Are the three of us really going after the book?"

"We'll need more than just us. We'll need five, six to be sure."

Rebecca nodded. "Multi person spell?" She remembered Salem saying something about only needing a small group.

"Yes." Twitch said. "You've learned about them yet?"

"Just about. If a spell is designed for more than two people, it's considered a multi person spell. The radius can be increased marginally by adding more people, but the cost will still be the same, magic wise, diminishing even more per mage added." Rebecca was literally reciting her class on the subject at this point. Twitch did not care, he merely nodded sagely.

"Indeed. We'll need to do a few different spells so it will be good to have people to switch in and out." He nodded and looked over. "It's a good strategy to avoid magic exhaustion."

Rebecca shivered and looked over.

"I heard it can be lethal."

"Oh no, only in very specific cases. Adult mages with some training generally never run such a risk." Twitch reassured. Rebecca picked up on something in that voice, a self confidence that only could have come from experience or age.

"So we should be fine?"

"Yes. Minor magic exhaustion leads to bloody noses, fatigue and fainting. As long as we look out for one another though, we will be fine." Twitch got up from the seat and made a face. "Ow. Getting old."

"Aren't you already?" Rebecca looked over with a chuckle. She found it hard to guess the man's age. He looked... mature, definitely, but the young face and his occasion facial tic namesake gave him a younger appearance.

Twitch merely chuckled.

"To get back to it, Rebecca. We will pick up a few more people. Lydia, she'll be really helpful for all kinds of scrying. She has a natural talent for it. Oh and Furcifer. The man with the biggest ego the world has ever seen."

"Isn't he the head of the Elites? Why would he want in on

some kind of treasure hunt?" Rebecca had heard the name being thrown around, but had not realised the man would be joining their team.

"Yeah, of the Elites. You're sharp." Twitch touched his nose. "Let's just say he owes me one."

Rebecca shrugged. Earlier that night there had been a lot of closed doors, nervous glances and long phone calls.

"Must be some favour." She said, looking over the books.

Twitch seemed to think for a moment.

"We better get some sleep." He threw a blanket over the sleeping man on the couch and walked up the stairs.

Chapter 37

From the moment Furcifer saw him, it was clear to him that Twitch had not expected this to last for so long. There were bags under his eyes and he had a certain slouch about him. It was time to head for the last book though. As long as they got that one, the majority of books was in their hands. He looked over the occupants of the large blue suv as it stopped near him.

"Hey. Get in." Twitch said, rolling down the window from the front passenger seat. He even sounded tired. The meeting place had been on neutral terrain, a car park ten minutes away from where he was staying. It was a pretty warm day- he had not expected Europe to be very warm, but he was getting away with a simple tshirt and jeans today.
"What a warm hello from-"

Twitch sighed. “I need your help. I don’t want it, but I need it.”
“Fine.” Furcifer opened up the door to the back seats and glanced over the gathered heads. There was a young lady, typing on her phone, sitting on the third of the middle row of seats and an older gentleman whom he recognised as Ethan was at the wheel.
“So you’re the infamous Atze Furcifer.”Ethan said.
Furcifer flapped his hand. “Yes yes. I am.” He sighed. “I'm not here to make friends.”
He said as the other held out his hand for a shake. He climbed in and plopped down next to the young lady.

“Who are you texting all the time anyway?” Furcifer turned to the girl.
“Nunya.” She said, raising an eyebrow.
“Yeah yeah, nunya business.” He rolled his eyes. “Alright.”

Twitch cleared his throat. “If everyone’s done arguing with Furcifer we can get started?” He shook his head...

Furcifer sighed and buckled up. “Alright. I’ll bite. What do we need to do?”
“Well, first we pick up Lydia.” Twitch looked around.
Furcifer groaned. The car would get crowded. Luckily, the air conditioning was keeping the temperature down.

Lydia was waiting near her house for the car, and jumped in happily.
"Hi!" She said enthusiastically, dimming at once when she caught sight of the dour mood in the van itself. "Gee, what a happy bunch..." She looked around.
Twitch chuckled. "Don't mind them."
"I know you." Furcifer looked over. "You were - ooh... You two..." He made a little finger motion between the two of them and Twitch groaned.
"Yes, we are seeing one another." Lydia said.
"Sorta dating." Twitch added. "I mean, right?"

Lydia glanced over and laughed. "Yes we are but this is not the best time to be discussing our relationship. Don't we have a world to save or something?" She tipped one of the middle seats and slipped into the back row.

"I like her." Furcifer nodded. "You know, now that she's not lying in my face." At that he whipped around to Twitch to glare at him. It seemed his anger was best directed at the sandy haired mage rather than his lovely companion.

"Oi. Behave." Twitch said to him, shaking his head. "She did what I asked her to do. You have an issue, take it up with me."
Furcifer narrowed his eyes. This would be the perfect time to kick it off. To just bring out all the doubts and hate he had in

his mind about this whole thing. The fact that he and Gabrielle were now pretty much under investigation. But... then this car would probably not go anywhere. He jerked his head back to the front and ran a hand through his hair to sleek it all back. He was tired, not just mentally but magically. This had to end for all of them before they became too worn out and started fighting among themselves even more. For once he decided he would be the bigger man, and looked at the expectant faces around him. They were staring, almost judging.

"Let's go." He shrugged.

Twitch nodded. "Alright. Glad we got there in the end." Twitch sat back. It was silent in the car, but anything was better than an all out shouting match in this rental.

Chapter 38

It was quiet for the longest time as they drove. It had been three hours since they left London and it would be at least another two before they even hit the Lake District. The dull monotone sound of the wheels on the asphalt almost rocked Twitch to sleep until Lydia cleared her throat. He quickly wiped his eyes to hide his sleepiness.

"So what will we be doing in the forest?" She broke the silence.

Twitch smiled. He'd expected the question and he was happy she had been the one to ask it. It would allow him to talk about it for a bit. Visualise the plan as it were. Also, he would seem like the smart one to her, which never hurt.

"We..." He cleared his throat. "We meet up with Salem."

This was assuming he had gotten the location right. Not a given considering he might be going on different data from Salem. It could be Salem had the wrong location, could be he had.

"If... When we find Salem we proceed with a ritual chant. Like a spell only longer." It was hard to speak about this stuff without making Lydia feel out of her depth.

"Okay. And that leads us to the book?" She said.

"So we hope. We are dealing with a lot of variables." Ethan licked his lips nervously.

Furcifer started awake from a nap. "It'll be a few hours before we get there, rest up." He stretched a little and looked around.

Lydia nodded and sat back, seemingly ok with his answers. He wished he was as well. To divert himself a little, he picked up the book Furcifer had brought in. He had let him join, but only if he got to look at the book the other had. It had some spliced in pages, with really interesting illustrations. They seemed much older than the book.

Furcifer looked over. "I have a theory the original seven based the Spell on a much older one. Or an older attempt at such a spell, at least." He nodded and looked over. "That's probably from the original source material, if so."

Twitch nodded. It was a wonderful illustration he had come across. A powerful looking mage who was looking around with a book in his arms. A few pages later, he was burying it.

"You think..." The hair on the back of his arms stood up. "That the one to make this spell before the seven, had hidden the books as well?"

"Not as good as Henrietta did, in that case." Rebecca remarked drily, putting her phone away and yawning.

Furcifer nodded. "She was one of the most successful mages of her time. It was only when she went after this spell that she became a bit of an outcast to be honest." He nodded and looked over.

Rebecca looked up. "She was quite something."

Ethan smiled a little. "She's still alive you know."

Twitch looked up. He knew many people thought she was no longer with them, but she was, and much sharper of mind than most half her age. He looked back down at the illustration. There was... something about it. In the end he shook his head before any spark of recognition could actually connect with his memories.

"So when do we get there?" He asked, turning towards Ethan.

"Just a few more hours, if traffic stays the same." He turned his head briefly but then turned back to mind the road. They'd been driving a quiet country road, but from time to time they would get stuck behind a farm tractor.

"We may not have much time until they find us there. Tell us what we'll need to do." Ethan said.

Twitch glanced over. "Ah. It's a first spell to be done with three people. It will likely wear us out so I suggest Furcifer, Ethan and I." That way they had other mages ready to take over magically if needed.

Furcifer sighed.

"Fine." He said, not so sure about Rebecca, it seemed. But he didn't care. Rebecca was on their side. She was the one Salem trusted and for some reason, that carried a lot of weight for him.

Three hours later, the car finally came to a halt. "We're here." Ethan said.

Chapter 39

The Lake District was beautiful, Twitch had to remark. It was one of the first times he'd ventured outside of London, but he hoped to do more of it. The forest was large, almost untouched looking, despite being right next to quite an extensive car park. It would be getting dark in a few hours, but there was still plenty of light. The air was crisp, and besides people getting into their cars to leave for home, there was a beautiful quiet in the air.

It had gotten colder the further they got from London - Lydia was hugging herself warm. As soon as the boot of the car opened, she dug into her bag for a sweater.

"Bit nippy huh?" She grinned and warmed her arms a bit. "Look at you. You okay?"

Twitch grinned a little.

"I'm alright. I'll grab my coat once Ethan has his stuff."

Lydia nodded, pulling the sweater over her head and tying a

parka around her waist.
It seemed they were all a bit out of their element here.
"Alright, if we're all ready to go. The park closes at five. This means we may have to use our commuter beads to get out of here." He said. The probability of that was increasing every minute. He looked around.
"In case you get separated, lost, whatever, use that bead. This forest is vast and unfamiliar." He said.

Ethan looked over. "Agreed. Does everyone have at least one bead?" He hoisted the backpack onto his back and took a deep breath, glancing around.
Furcifer climbed out last, and put a scarf around his neck, glancing around.
"Jeeze. This looks almost desolate."
"What better place to hide something?" Ethan grinned.
Twitch sighed and took his coat out of the boot before locking the car.
Rebecca turned to Ethan.
"I don't have any beads." She cleared her throat, and Ethan fished out two to give to her.
"This one's for King's Cross, the other is for Liverpool Street." He explained to her, and she nodded, putting them on her necklace.
"Thanks." She smiled a little.

"Let's get this show on the road. It's taken us long enough to get here." The redhead grumped.

Twitch couldn't help but chuckle. They were getting closer!

"There he is." Ethan sounded wary as they saw a figure approach.

Rebecca grinned. "Hi Salem!" She called out.

Salem sped up as Rebecca called out, apparently reassured by the youth's presence. Twitch was glad they'd brought her along, but it was still a responsibility to have the young woman there. Hopefully everything went as planned.

Furcifer raised an eyebrow and looked to Twitch. "He's coming? What's he doing here?"

"Long story." Said Twitch. "He's got knowledge we need."

Salem caught up and nodded to them. "So you are serious about doing this?" He asked Twitch.

Twitch frowned.

"Yes, yes I am." He looked at him. Was he worried he was not serious enough about this?

"You can still quit."

A chill ran down his spine.
"Excuse... me?" There was a note in the man's voice which he did not like.
"You can still get back into that car and stop it. Nobody will think worse of you."
"No!" Twitch reacted strongly. "No. Not at all." He sighed and looked away.
"Let's get on with it. I'm quite ready to call this a day."

And from Furcifer's face, he could see the other was quite ready to go as well.
Lydia smiled encouragingly.

"Come on! It'll get dark soon." Twitch said, walking off towards the edge of the forest.
"Yeah, let's go." Ethan glanced at Salem, who took in a deep breath. It seemed the two still weren't quite on trusting terms, but that was alright. In a few hours, hopefully, they could all go their separate ways. He punched coordinates into his gps. It wouldn't be very precise, but it would get them close enough to find the book without magical means.

Chapter 40

Furcifer hissed as another twig hit him in the face.
"I wouldn't have guessed there was this much wildlife in the UK." He mocked, swatting at a midge. His joke fell flat. Even Twitch did not look up. He sighed. Lydia, whom he had pegged as a city dweller, made her way through the bushes much faster than he. He constantly found his sweater catching on branches and twigs.

"How much further?"
Twitch looked over. "Until we reach the clearing, then we regroup." He said, looking around the group.

Furcifer followed his gaze. Rebecca was keeping up surprisingly well despite the uneven terrain. In fact even with her stumbling from time to time they were making good time, but the terrain was quite easy so far. That could change at any moment and he knew it. By now it was after five, the park would be closing. Hopefully they would not run into any patrols or anything. It would be hard to explain to a park ranger what they were doing out here.

The shadows finally let up as they reached the clearing. Immediately it was warmer and drier, and Furcifer welcomed the change.

However he knew that to get into the open space meant that they were visible and vulnerable. He peered around nervously.

"We'll stop at the edge of the clearing." Twitch decided, peeking down at his gps unit.

Furcifer nodded This was tiring. The forest walk and keeping everyone together were taxing the short man, much more used to following than leading. It also seemed they were being lead up a hill.

Furcifer looked over to Twitch.
They needed him now. Whenever he looked around, he saw him fumbling with notes and books, so he was confident he would get to that soon enough. Salem did not seem very happy, but he was trudging along. Ever since the exchange between the two of them at the edge of the forest, they had both seemed very on edge. Salem had seemingly told the other to just give up on his quest.

Furcifer wondered what that was about - wouldn't he have been excited to share in this adventure? It wasn't every day that they uncovered one of the biggest spells in the history of magic. Personally, he was quite excited to be part of the group who puzzled it all together, even if they were rushed in doing so to make sure it didn't fall into the wrong hands. And had betrayed eachother in their quest. And had - his train of thought was disturbed by twigs giving way.

Twitch rushed to the front, squeezing past Furcifer.
"So uh, we uh, we can cross the clearing and then we head... south. Doesn't look like the layout of the forest has changed much, so we might just get there before the sun is even down." He smiled a little.
The trek was making him sweaty and tired, but Furcifer was glad to see some signs of initiative.

Furcifer returned to his train of thought.

Fact, Salem had been alive for a very long time.

Fact, Twitch had previously lived in an ages centuries.

Fact, the spell had been based on an older manuscript's work.

What if they knew each other better than they were letting on?

A shiver ran down his spine.

Chapter 41

Twitch looked around to see where Lydia was. Even if he was having a hard time keeping up, he was not doing it to impress her. He was really just trying to end this whole thing before he had no physical energy or mental stamina left. Branches swept by his legs and arms, and he had sprained his ankle a few miles ago - nevertheless he kept pushing on, hobbling if he had to.

Shortly after the start of this journey, he had casts some spells on himself to keep focussed and energetic. He had to stay alert and with it right now. It needed to end today so he could just get on with his life, without it falling into the wrong hands.

After another few minutes of hiking, the clearing came into view. Ethan caught up, only a little out of breath.
"Hah. We didn't even do this much hiking back when we camped together." Ethan grinned and looked around.
Twitch grinned back. Those had been good memories -

perhaps the first time since being resurrected where he had been alone with another person. Ethan had taught him how to roast marshmallows, even though he had been the older and taller one of the two back then.

"Yeah. We should do that again some time."

"After all of this is over." Ethan concurred.

"Yeah." Twitch raised an arm. "Stay here." He said before walking towards the open ground of the claring. It did not seem like they had been followed. Hopefully the Guild had given up on them. It must have been confusing to any onlookers. Their group had split up, rejoined, split up again. Hard to keep up.

It was quiet for a while as Twitch scouted ahead and for a few minutes, he was acutely aware of every rustling leaf and every snapping twig.

He returned to the group a little later.

"It's safe." He nodded. "Let's take a rest and regroup."

He looked around the gaggle of people gathered. Rebecca had taken out her phone and was trying to find a signal, while Ethan put down his backpack. Lydia was hanging back with Furcifer, sharing some sunscreen . It was quite funny to see the redhead roll up his pants to apply the lotion, while Lydia gracefully rubbed her shoulders down. When she caught him looking, she winked.

He blushed and looked away. A rock under his feet almost unbalanced him as he tried to take a few casual steps away.
Furcifer rolled his eyes and shook his head, engaging in some small talk with Lydia.

Twitch cleared his throat and regained his composure somewhat.
They were quite the team. Some very talented mages and some... not so much.
But they would have to do.
Ethan snorted at his display and shook his head before turning serious again.

"Twitch. So we go south?"
"Yes." He nodded, wiping some sweat off his brow. "South until the grand yew."
"A grand yew. I just hope it hasn't been cut down yet." Furcifer sighed, before swatting at a midge.
"Those should be the least of your worries." Lydia said, looking over to him. "We're following an ancient map here."
She looked vigilant, careful with every step.
"Not a map. A poem." Twitch said dully.

"That's not much better." Said Rebecca, putting the phone away.

"This place doesn't even show up on google maps."

"I know where we're going, okay?" Twitch said with a frown. "You can stop doubting me, all of you!" He was getting frustrated.

"Gee, I'm sorry." Rebecca frowned. "It's just that it's getting late. That's all."

Twitch shook his head and glanced up to the sky. The sun was lowering, he could feel the temperature dropping. The longer they were out here the more dangerous it became. Navigating back in the dark would prove hard, and to portal away with a book of unknown magic was not the best outcome for this situation. He got the group moving again, trying not to be spooked by the sounds of wildlife coming from all around them.

Ethan grinned. "You've become quite the city dweller. You used to tell me which birds made which calls."

"I was making it up." Twitch admitted drily. "I have no idea what Goosefilled Downbirds sound or look like."

"Aha. I now know that one's made up at least." Ethan grinned and walked a few steps backwards with him. Twitch couldn't help but chuckle, even though his mood had greatly soured. They needed to find this thing soon.

The open clearing made way to a more difficult patch, filled with younger trees and twigs fighting for sunlight. Their feet regularly sunk into patches of mud, and it was noticeably colder without the sunlight filtering through. After about fifteen minutes of the difficult trek, they reached a much larger clearing than the one they had seen before.

"So, where - is... that it?" Lydia's pupils dilated as the sun was blocked out by the shadow of a large tree appearing into view.

The large yew tree cast its shadow into the open area and over Lydia's face. Its branches just sprawled over the shorter trees beneath it, which had been denied the sunlight. It stood proudly past the open area, about ten meters away. Its trunk was almost a metre in diameter, and its many branches sprawled, mirroring the many roots it had burrowed into the ground.

"That's it." Twitch shivered. He had seen this tree before, he realised with a shiver. Had it been here long enough for him to have known it from his life long, long ago? He shook his head. Perhaps it was just a familiar sight. Deja vu. He'd been to plenty of forests on his travels. That had to be it. He tried to shake the feeling as they hiked over to the tree. Perhaps Ethan and he had just camped in a similar forest once, long ago.

Once he had gone to Siberia to see a local mage for a few ingredients, and the man had taken him to the place of the Tunguska explosion. It had been an awe-inspiring sight but it had not felt as ominous, as strange as this place. The hairs on the back of his neck rose. It was strange, yet somehow so familiar. He blamed it on the spells he had placed upon himself to stay energetic and sound of mind. Of course it would affect his senses a bit. He shook his head.

It took him a moment to gather himself before he walked over to the tree and placed his hand on it. At first he had thought he would have to remember some kind of spell or he would have to wait for it to come. Instead, it interrupted him while he thought, coming over him.

The spell came without any false starts. It came from deep within, where his magic was, and in a sing song tone sounding eerily like a lullaby. He felt his heart slowing and a deep calm spreading over him as he listened to those tones, feeling so different by virtue of bone conduction. The vibrations seemed to be the real magic in this spell.

Twitch's voice deepened as it got to the end of the spell, and at the end, he opened his eyes and removed his slightly sweaty palm. Briefly, he flexed his fingers before wiping his hand on the seat of his pants.

"That's about it..." His voice came through hoarse and be cleared his throat. He looked around as if he was trying to remember where he was.

Salem looked very worried, taking a few large steps back. Twitch had noticed that the old soul was restless ever since they had crossed the open space.

"Are you alright?" He asked Salem softly, reaching an arm out to him. Likewise, Lydia strode over with a bottle of water.

"Drink something. You look..." She shook her head. "You haven't been drinking enough water for a trek like this."

Salem looked over and blinked, but before he could answer the tree rotated softly. It did not look mechanical but natural - it was as if the yew itself had decided to twist around. As it turned, a row of text became visible, etched into the bark.

"Holy fuck... A spell grown into a tree." Furcifer said, rushing over to examine it. The rest was a bit more hesitant. Rebecca kept her distance, biting her lip as if she was expecting the thing to suddenly break out in a loud noise. Ethan stayed back as well, looking on from afar.

Salem looked back to Rebecca, making sure the young woman was alright before looking back. "Don't touch it!" He warned.

Furcifer frowned. "It's just a spell. Etta hid it."

"The Spell we're chasing is not just a spell. This does not seem like her style. Honestly. It is..." Ethan said..

"Too advanced for her to have done as a young mage." Furcifer finished her thought. "Maybe she got someone to help?" He looked up to Twitch and Salem, as if expecting a reaction.

"I don't think she did." Ethan said softly. "Not her style to leave a clue like this. She was all about the portability - what if it's a trap?"

“It’s not a trap.” Salem shook his head. “This is where you will need all the manpower we’ve brought.” He looked at the spell, reaching out as if tempted to run his fingers over it.“I can’t read it. It’s ancient.”

Furcifer sat down to take notes."She did leave traps. One of the books turned out to be a Mimic. Twitch fought a spider. I would be careful.” He glanced at Salem. “Unless you know more about this specific one?”

Lydia smiled. “I know this! It's English. Middle English?” She glanced at Furcifer. Twitch brushed aside a pang of jealousy.
“Salem?”
“I can't read it.” Salem shrugged. “Not anymore, at least.”
Furcifer looked up at Lydia.
“Guess it's up to us to translate then. It’s Old English, but it’s easy enough to translate. You can tell because there are no w’s. It’s only a little older than the spells I stole from Twitch’s books.”
“Rude.” Twitch sighed. “I wrote those, you know.”
Furcifer waved a hand. “Yes yes. And I published them while you hoarded them.”

"Was that before or after you became head of a Faction and betrayed us all?" Twitch crouched down near the man and ran his hand over the spell. "Ah... This seems very familiar."
"And that's what I don't like." Salem kneeled down by him. "Twitch. You can still leave. We can take it from here."
"What?" Twitch frowned, whipping his head towards the other. "I've come all this way for it!"
"Doesn't mean you're entitled to it."

Furcifer looked up. "Hold up. I'm confused. What is this about, Salem? He was the product of this spell and he is the closest to Etta! How is he not entitled to it?"
Twitch wanted to hear this as well. He raised an eyebrow at the man.
Salem sighed but ignored Furcifer.
"Asa. You have to remember this." He said, looking over to his friend. "You asked me, begged me to keep you from finding this out."
Twitch went wide eyed. "Salem. You know who I was?"
"I was your friend. Way back when in 1500." The sadness in Salem's eyes was real. In those brown eyes... he could tell he had seen them before. So very long ago. Salem reached out and touched him, and he could feel that familiar prickle of magic, not unlike what he had transferred to Lydia to spark her powers.

His hand shot to his mouth, dulling a surprised gasp. "Salem? Oh god." The soft magic touch brought back images, flashes. He had known this man as a friend, many years ago. Images came back to him, dulled by the mental sharpening spells, but nonetheless real. The two of them had worked, crafted spells, discovering the limits of their magic. Walking together through this - this place, back when it had been a forest, not just a patchy woodland. A cabin in the woods. Making their marks on the world around them.

Salem nodded. "The story Etta told you was never correct. She didn't know any better than to paint you as a sweet innocent boy living in the middle ages before you died. But you were not. You were fully aware of the extent of your power. And when you realised they were coming for you... The witch hunters..."
"... I asked your help in writing a reviving spell. In case I was executed." Shaking now, he took a few paces and crouched down. "And I hid the spell somewhere around here. That's why Etta lead us back to it. To remind me."
"You asked me to use it but I had to leave town." Salem

continued. "After a while I lost track of where the book was buried. I couldn't find it again and..." He shook his head. "At that point I thought it might be best to leave you dead. Your power would have outgrown you if you had continued on that path. Which is why I don't think you should have this last book."
Twitch shivered. "I... I'm so sorry. But it should not fall into other hands, either."

It all made so much sense now. Much more - Etta would never have written such a spell on her own, or even with a group. She had mentioned the journal in her letter, perhaps that was why she had wanted him to read it.
It fit better than anything else. She had definitely improved upon the original. He remembered how much pain the initial spell would have caused. Theoretically - he had never gotten to test it.

Furcifer blinked. "You - you planned your own revival?"
"It seems I did..." Twitch nodded.
Furcifer shot up. "You son of a bitch! This -you created this? This is one of the most lethal spells in the magic world! Magic should never be used for such selfish purposes or to meddle

with life and death!"
The notebook tumbled off of his lap, falling down and closing neatly on the forest floor.
Lydia took a deep breath. He couldn't quite tell how she was feeling - perhaps he was just too absorbed by his own pain right now. She paced, hands to her mouth. The sound of Furcifer's rage came from far away, even though the man was just a metre or two away.

Ethan sighed. "We need to get on with it. If the IMG catches up with us, it's game over, especially if we're all here in a nice, easy to capture package."
"You really think...? Nevermind, we're talking about immortality here." Furcifer shrugged.
"He's right. No telling what they might do." Rebecca said softly.
There was no telling what anyone would do for such a power. Twitch heard Furcifer calm down, his breathing evening out.

"Come on. We need to do this spell. Is everyone still okay with this?" Furcifer looked around. "We can find the last notebook and put it to rest."
Rebecca nodded. "I'll help." Twitch guessed she just wanted to get home at this point, from the amount of time she spent trying to get connection on her phone. Her parents probably worried.

Lydia got up. “I’m still in. For what that’s worth. I trust you.”
“That’s worth a lot. I’m in.” Nodded Salem. “Only if we destroy this.”
Furcifer threw his head back. “Fine! But I agree with destroying this!” He said, crossing his arms.

The wind kicked up as a large circle of bright light appeared. It formed a portal, through which Manon appearedm looking panicked.
Manon looked around, dressed in a pair of jeans and a casual shirt with a cardigan over it.

“Sorry! Sorry! I know you told me not to come but there is news from the IMG, they took-” She looked around and blinked.
“Oh fish. I fell for it. They put out this big thing about how they had grabbed Twitch...” Seeing Twitch, she paused. “What? They didn't grab you?”
“Where did you learn that news?” Ethan shot up.
“I uh, there was something... On the TV...”
“And you portaled here straight away.” Furcifer rubbed the bridge of his nose.
“Security on the spell?”
“Very little.” She squeaked. “I was in a hurry.”
“They might have traced it then. We need to keep moving.”

He sighed.
This whole situation was far from ideal.
Twitch shook his head. "Let's have a seat and regroup."
The silence was palpable. Furcifer threw his hands up and sighed.
"We can't rest now! We're-"
"I know, but I need time!" Twitch barked. His whole world had been turned upside down.
"I need a break from this." He shook his head and walked off towards the bushes. The others were left in silence, but everyone else just sat down, not bothering to go after him.

Twitch looked over to Manon, who looked ready to go after him, and shook his head. It was best to let him wander a bit.
"We've got about five minutes. Then we move." He shook his head. They were sitting ducks but without Furcifer, he could not go on with this.
Salem was looking everywhere but the spell and he himself was only just starting to pull himself together. He was unfocused and taking the break had been a bad decision, but it was done now.
Furcifer was eager to take the lead and he couldn't let him do that. This was his mission, his history. The redhead was only here to help him. All that was left to be done was to pick up the last book... his... journal, and go home.

"Thanks for joining, Manon. It's good to have someone spare." He was watching her, fussing as she tried to figure whether to leave or stay.
She looked up and smiled. "Good. You guys have this cute girl in your gang I wouldn't mind spending some time with."
Rebecca grinned at that, briefly looking up from the straps of the backpack she was messing with.

Ethan looked up. "I got a translation. It's rudimentary..."
"It will do." Twitch took the notebook from him and read it through. As he had feared, he recognised most of it. His stomach made a painful drop as he cleared his throat. No turning back now. After all they'd been through that, giving up would be even worse than failing. At least if they failed, he had made an attempt to set things right again.
"Alright, this should help us find it... Where is everyone."

Manon threw her hands in the air and walked over to find Furcifer.
"Where the hell is he now?"

Chapter 42

There had been another reason Twitch had been unwilling to pause. He was not sure if he would manage to will himself back to his feet after this. If they had walked for another ten minutes maybe he would have been in a better place.

Twitch wondered if he looked as broken as he felt. All this time he had thought he was a good person who was living his life as best he could. To have that pulled out from under him was painful, devastating. He had never been that good person. He had been a scheming, evil mage who had caused the deaths of at least four good mages. Who knows how many others had attempted this spell, emboldened by what Henrietta and the others had done? He swallowed and tried to get his mind back on track. He had to lead them to this last book and then it would be over.

Lydia approached him.

"Hi." He looked up from the lines he was drawing in the dirt.

"Quite the mess huh?" She smiled a little.

He nodded. "Mmm." He said. "I wish things had gone differently. I do."

"It's... over with." She sighed and sat down next to him. So what do we do next?"

"Once the spell is translated, we just follow it to the book. That's basically it. It's hidden in an old tree, kind of like the earlier spell."

"That's quite the treasure hunt."

"It's an important book." He said, looking over to her. "It has the core of the spell, the part it's all built from. All spells have a core, and with that core you determine the action of your magic. The rest is just details, things that can be filled in if you try hard enough. Of course it works best with all original parts." He said. "If they had gotten this one rather than the

other one..." He shook his head.
"Right. Furcifer told me they had gotten one of the books already." She nodded. "So inside this book there is a single spell, that works together with one spell in six other books... That's a dizzying amount of combinations."
"It's meant to be safe." Twitch got up. "And then people decided to try and find it anyway. This system was set up way back when." He sighed.

"It will be safest once we've destroyed everything."
Lydia nodded slowly. "I see." She got up and looked over. "We're close now. Before the end of the day, we'll have it."

Suddenly a shot rang out.
Twitch gasped. His ears were ringing and his heart felt like it was about to explode. It felt like the world was going in slow motion as he turned his head to look at Ethan, who had sagged to his knees.

Even from here he could see it was too late. He rushed over but he couldn't - Ethan's hand slipped away from his own and he sagged to his knees.
He whipped around to see where the shot had come from.
Quentin stood in the clearing, aiming the gun down.

Twitch felt a pain in his stomach, and realised he was about to throw up. He turned away from Ethan's body and threw up on the forest floor.
Lydia put an arm on his shoulder, looking shell shocked. He had not felt great about himself before any of this but now? He felt like dying.
Rebecca screamed, and only Salem putting his arms around her calmed her down a little. Manon was staring, wide eyed.

"Now that I have your attention." Quentin said coolly. "I think you are all aware that I'm here for the spell, so now that we have that out of the way."
Twitch struggled to breathe in- he was hyperventilating. They had run out of time and - there was nothing he could do. Furcifer looked on coolly, calculating, and in that moment Twitch hated him more than anything.
"So, where is my book?"
"It's not yours!" Said Manon, standing up defiantly. "You -you can't!"
Twitch wiped his mouth and got up. "Where is Furcifer." He asked.

"I ran into him in the woods while he was... relieving himself, so I knocked him out." He shrugged. "I'll let the girls go and get him." He nodded to Manon and Rebecca.
"Come on." He said, looking over to them. "He's near the bushes there." He pointed out, and even Twitch could see the redhead in the grass from there.
Rebecca shivered but held a hand out to Manon, walking towards the unconscious Furcifer.

"We won't give you the book." Said Manon defiantly.
"Really now?" Quentin chuckled.
"F... Furcifer was translating the spell." Said Twitch, looking around for the man's notebook and noticing he was still dizzy. Damn.
"I - I'll need to finish translating it." He cleared his throat and looked at where Furcifer had left off. It looked like there wasn't much left to be done, which was a massive relief.
"How long?" Quentin asked.
"Fifteen minutes. Why-Why did you shoot Ethan?"
"He betrayed me." Quentin said, as if that was the most logical thing in the world. The leader had come prepared - he was wearing wellies, cotton trousers and a parka against mud and rain. And possibly blood, Twitch thought grimly.
"Now come on. Get the book out of its hiding place and we can get started."
"Started with what?" Groaned Salem. "You won't be able to

use the spell either way."
"And I'd hate to end your long life, Salem. You could still join us and reach the highest ranks."
"No thanks." Salem laughed and looked over. "I'd rather die." He spat at Quentin, who just shrugged.
"Try that again and the girl gets it." Said Quentin, and Twitch saw Salem shift his gaze towards Rebecca.
"Alright. Alright." Twitch raised a hand. He needed to make something happen.

Their options were limited. They still had to find the book and then get out of here. Ethan's loss... He would have to mourn later.
But to get the book they would have to go through Quentin and he did not like that idea at all. Furcifer was probably the strongest mage out of all of them and he was currently drooling on the floor. Maybe if he could get back up... But even so, the spell on Furcifer could not last for a long time. Quentin was getting older.

"Alright. Put the gun away. You can't do much with just the book so... I'll let you take it. That's it."
"And the other books?"
"I can't give them to you." Twitch shook his head. "I gave them to Furcifer and he took them to his Faction." He lied. Furcifer could not deny or confirm anything anyway. He took a deep breath as he looked over to Quentin, to see how he would react.

Quentin glanced back at Furcifer, who was being dragged over to the group. Twitch walked over and checked the man's vital signs.
"You two okay?" Asked Twitch.
Manon nodded. "Yeah. He's so freaking heavy though!" She put her hands on her sides and sighed.

Quentin looked over. “Finish up that spell. I want the book.”

Twitch groaned. “Alright. Alright.”

“I may even let you use it to bring back your brother.” Said Quentin, but it did not make him feel any better. He shook his head and took the notebook to finish up the translation. Lydia joined him, sitting down near him.

“What are we doing?” She whispered.

“We're biding time.” He answered, looking back down to the notepad.

“I'm almost done.” He announced a little louder.

“Alright.” Salem walked over and looked over to the spell, trying to ignore Quentin. It was clear he had not signed up for this and that he wanted to get out of here.

“We need to do this spell at the old tree.” He said, looking from the spell to Twitch.

“Mm. I know. It'll take us a bit to get there with Furce out.” He said, shivering a little. The sun was going down. Earlier they had worried about patrols when the park closed, but now Twitch kind of hoped someone would come by. Stop this whole thing. Ethan's body nearby was a chilling reminder - this could end very badly for all of them and he had to admit he was scared.

He almost wished Gabrielle was here. She could actually put up a fight against Quentin.

“Let's go. I know where we're going.” Said Twitch, getting up. Could they really leave Ethan here? He swallowed down tears. It was real. Ethan hadn't moved. Someone would find his body. He would be treated as a John Doe.

☆ ☆ ☆

The chill really hit them and it was becoming hard to navigate without any light. Quentin had a torch on him and Manon was lighting the way with a magical orb, but it would only get harder from here on as they entered a denser part of the forest.

“This is the tree. I need five people touching it before we say the spell together. It's fine. It's short.” He passed the notebook Lydia, who handed it on after memorising it.

At this point he could see Furcifer shifting on his own from time to time, a good sign. But even Quentin would soon realise that his spell’s effect could not have lasted that long. In fact the man did look a little more on edge. With the thick canopy above them, it was very likely he had no contact with his back up. It was something they could easily use against him.

Twitch nodded. “We all touch in succession, then recite the spell.” Twitch said. “And if everything went as it should, then it will reveal to us the book’s location.” As he said it he heard himself calm down. Knowing the near future brought such comfort. And knowing they were almost there was even better.

Quentin organised them back into a tight group. “The spell now.” He said, not joining in with the spellcasting. Probably smart, Twitch thought. He was conserving his own energy to keep Furcifer under as long as possible.

Twitch took a deep breath. “Alright.” He nodded and started off, the rest of the group joining. The spell was only eight words long, but it felt like the longest spell in his life.

Behind him, Furcifer was stirring. Hopefully, he would be okay to move after this spell. Manon was helping him sit up.

“It’s short.” Frowned Quentin.

“It’s just a location spell.” Salem defended. “It's fine.”

Twitch nodded. “He’s right. It is just a locating spell, like... Scrying.” He wiped his hands on his pants.

“And now what?”

“Now we wait.” Salem looked to Quentin and sat down.

Chapter 43

The shade of the trees had shifted before Manon got up.
"It's been twenty minutes. It didn't work." Manon said, looking to Quentin. Like most in the group, she seemed to be blaming the man. Quentin simply raised an eyebrow, aware the group was tense.
"If this is an attempt to sabotage..." He started.
Twitch got up. "Sabotage what? The spell didn't work because you are here.You are an intruder and the magic recognised that."
Twitch shivered. Maybe it did not work with too many people present. Maybe it had not worked with an odd number. It could have been any number of things. Maybe it didn't work with only four active magic users.

"The magic recognises nothing." Quentin shot up up and looked over Twitch.
"You, get me that book or something nasty will happen to your girl." He pointed menacingly at Lydia, but turned into a strange blur as he was tackled by Furcifer.

The red haired mage was clearly unstable on his feet, but held on to Quentin easily, trying to bring him down to the ground with his weight. Quentin pushed back against the man and stood his ground.

Manon jumped up and uttered a spell to immobilise the older man before crouching down by Furcifer. She grabbed the gun from the man and prepared another spell.

Quentin dodged easily and blinked. "You're fast for an old man!"

He knocked Furcifer aside. "Now... Behave." He pressed a button on a device he produced from his pocket.

Furcifer growled, and went for him again. This time, Quentin had no time to dodge both the spell and his attacker.

Manon's spell came fast, hard.

This time, the Faction leader went down like a brick.

"We got him!" Lydia gasped, looking over as he fell. "He did something though..."

She grabbed the device that was still in the man's hands.

"I don't think it's a detonator." She sighed, turning the item he had activated over in his hands.

Manon gasped, suddenly realising she was holding a gun, and dropped it into the grass.

Furcifer got up with a groan. “Good. What an ass.” He slurred, leaning against Manon
Twitch sighed. “He won’t be able to call for help, but we can’t leave him here.”

Manon looked up. “This is a transmitter of some sort. He’s already called for help.”
Salem nodded. “I can transport him back to the guild but they’ll be here in five minutes to get us.”
“I vote we leave him here until we get the book.” Manon huffed. “And if that thing was a tracker, taking him will only give away our location.”
“If we get the book.” Rebecca looked around. “That tree was supposed to tell us where it is. It’s been thirty minutes now.”
“You’re right.” Twitch said, sitting down.

Salem sat down with him. “Perhaps it’s for the best. If we can’t get it...”
“Quentin can come back here tomorrow with enough mages to do the spell. What if it works for him then?” Twitch got up.
“No, we need to find it now. We have two and a half hours left.” He was not even mentioning Ethan - that was still too painful. The man would not be found until the next morning.

"Fine. We're taking him with us and we'll let him go when we have the book. Maybe after subjecting him to a little confusion spell." Lydia grinned and broke the device she'd examined in two before throwing it behind her back.

"We're not dragging him with us!" Furcifer groaned.
"I dragged your useless ass along, Furcifer." Manon looked over to him.
Salem sighed.
"Let's focus on the main issue here. How do we find the book?"
"Maybe..." Lydia cleared her throat. "Maybe I can find it."
Salem chuckled. "What makes you think..."
"It's a scrying spell right? That's what you need. They're my speciality." She insisted.
Manon looked to Twitch, who nodded.

"Hey, it'll be fine." Manon smiled encouragingly. "You're a pro at these spells and you've got good intentions. In magic, that counts more than anything."

"You mean more than skill?" She chuckled nervously.

"No. It's just a spell and you are more than capable. I trust that, or Twitch wouldn't have brought you along."

Lydia took a deep breath and grabbed a piece of paper to note down spell bits. She had learned basic spell formation in the mean time, enough for scrying spells at least.

"I can do this. Yeah." She looked to Twitch.

Twitch smiled and gave her a thumbs up. She nodded back and started the spell, one hand over the pages as she chanted the spell. It was a lot less imposing sounding than other spells that day, but Twitch remained vigilant. The group spells had cost them all magic and she would be near exhaustion at this point. Especially after the offensive spells being hurled around, they needed to be careful. She pushed through a hard part and took a deep breath after finishing it.

"Follow me." Was all she said.
The group broke through the low foliage and followed Lydia. Twitch peeked back often to make sure that Furcifer was still following and that Manon hadn't left Quentin in a tree. They were all growing tired after the long day, and it was noticeable from the pace. Furcifer was still slow, still recovering from the spell that had immobilised him for the better part of an hour. Walking a little faster, Twitch caught up with Lydia. While her pace was also slowed by fatigue and the branches they were breaking through, she moved with purpose, direction.

"Hey."
"Hey." She replied, looking briefly in his direction before looking forward again. "We're so close." There was a note of frustration in her voice.
"Can you pinpoint it? Or just a direction?" Twitch steered.
Manon rushed up. "It's okay. Just stop until you feel it again."
She had helped many a budding mage come into their powers and she knew how to help them out when a spell was frustrating them.

Lydia paused and looked around before taking a deep breath of the cooling forest air.
"That way." She headed down a forked path and lead them to an open spot, before taking off again, down a little old

mud path, which had once been trodden much more frequently.
Twitch went wide eyed. Somehow, it was.... Familiar. He paused, biting his lip as he took in the scenery. He had formed memories here, he was sure of it. When he snapped out of his contemplation, he could see Salem doing a very similar thing.
"You know this place?"
Salem nodded. "I do." He looked over. "It was near my first cabin. Feels like it was a lifetime ago."
"Lifetimes, in your case." Furcifer uttered before breaking through the last few branches.
Salem sighed before turning back to Twitch. "Remember, whatever happens... You are still you."
"Found it!" Lydia called out, crouching down by a rock and rolling it off of its resting place, before wiping some dirt off. A fabric wrapped package came up, and her small hands quickly unwrapped the book before letting Twitch take her place.

"Is that it?" Manon looked over. As Twitch nodded shakily, she snapped her fingers to set Quentin free, before casting a quick spell on him. Twitch couldn't hear what it was, but it was most likely a confusion spell.

The journal of Asa Ward, it read in bold, embossed letters. Asa swallowed hard and leaned back against the tree. It made his stomach turn to see this again.

"This is all my fault. I started all this bloodshed, all this chaos." He said softly, sliding down into a crouch to hug his knees.
"I cost so many people their lives..."
Salem sat down by him.
"I didn't want you to find this out. When you had just returned... You were as mean as you were before but you didn't remember anything. Etta's care mellowed you and you became... happy. Happier than you had ever been. I wanted you to have that second chance." He said softly, putting a hand on his shoulder.
"You need to destroy this journal, Asa. You were bolder and more competent than Furcifer. If these spells see the light of day..." Salem sounded serious.

"But... " Asa looked at the book. This had been his life before all this. This would help him remember all of it. He looked to Salem and shook his head. However little he remembered, ever since he had met this man, he remembered that trust between them. Even beyond memories there was a bond he could not ignore.
"For you, Ethan." He whispered.

Salem sighed in relief. "Thank you, Asa."
"Not Asa." He reached over to take Lydia's hand. " I'm Twitch now." He said, picking up the book with his other hand. Yes. He would destroy the book now, that was the best thing. Now that there was a moment to think... He realised that would be what Ethan would have wanted, more than anything. In his mind, he finished up the spell to turn it into dust, unaware he had triggered a magic countdown.

Chapter 44

Furcifer felt the air being forced from his lungs, and he struggled to fill them again. His muscles were still stiff from the long paralysis, and rolling away was a challenge.

The book's resting place had been a trap, and they hadn't even noticed.

Ten seconds after Twitch had unwrapped the book, there had been a large blast. Furcifer had tried to stay upright, but he was slammed into a tree.

Grass and patches of dirt flew around, and the ground shook noticeably. A low murmur went through the ground. The sky went dark. At first, Furcifer thought it had been because of the dust thrown up, but the sun had, in what seemed a matter of seconds, traversed the sky. It had become the middle of the night almost instantaneously. A timelapse spell - the sort of thing that would send a medieval man running in fear.

Rebecca grabbed Manon and ducked low to the ground, as if expecting another blow. Salem had fared no better as he was thrown to the ground, clambering to get back up again. Rebecca pulled Manon closer, and somehow he knew there was screaming, but he was unable to hear it.

Twitch and Lydia had caught the worst of it - they were not moving, probably knocked out by the initial blast. Salem was not moving either, and the tree nearest to them was falling. There was a loud audible creak as the tree's trunk gave way. Twitch, Lydia and Salem were in its path.

Furcifer yelled out, but his voice did not make any noise. Or maybe it did, and he just didn't hear it. He scrambled up, palms scratched and bloodied as he rushed over and uttered a spell to keep the tree from falling. It half worked - it diverted the tree. With a loud bang, it fell to the side, only inches away from Salem's head. As he fell back to his knees, he saw the three were safe. Salem slowly raised his head, but then squeezed his eyes shut. Something was terribly off. Even now, almost a full minute after the spell blast, they hadn't recovered yet. This spell was old, ancient, and very very powerful. He glanced at Twitch.

There was a loud thudding sound, and for a moment, Furcifer wondered if it was his heartbeat. He looked up and saw a helicopter approach, going past them at first, but then turning. A patrol? A large search light shone over the area and the helicopter descended. It was a small, light looking helicopter, in a navy blue that seemed almost black, with a logo on the tail.

Finally, it seemed to decide on a spot and descended swiftly, the blades of the helicopter
The engines seemed to be going on for the longest time.
Rebecca jumped up and waved her arms. Salem grabbed her and pulled her down.
"You idiot! It's the IMG." He said, though again he could not hear himself. The logo was quite clear now and he pointed at it, hoping to at least get his point across that way.

This was not a police helicopter. Now that it had landed, he could feel the tremors the strong engine caused. It did not seem like they planned to stay for long.

Some jumped out, easily gathering the stunned seekers. Furcifer hardly had enough energy to resist as he too was pushed into a helicopter. The last thing he saw was one of the men walking over to the tree stump to pick up the book, only seconds before the helicopter jolted off the ground.

Chapter 45

Twenty eight. Twenty nine. Thirty. Twitch stopped pacing.

And now they were all here, in a small cell, about thirty steps around. He had paced around the small room for the last two days now.

He barely remembered the helicopter. He remembered Furcifer running at him, and the tree falling, and then someone picked him up.

They were being held - that was for sure.The cell, for a better word of it, was gray and small. He could hear pipes behind the wall, but they were too thick to hear anything beyond that.
The small rooms were well equipped, and three times a day a tray of food would appear through a slot in the door. There was a small bathroom in every cell, hidden behind a frosted glass sliding door, and a futon. Not exactly a sensory scintillating environment but it was comfortably survivable. He rubbed a hand through his hair and sat down on the futon.

He had measured the passage of time by the trays of food coming in and the artificial light, which was turned off every day, about three hours after the dinner tray came, and came back on about an hour before breakfast arrived. On the second day, they had shoved a change of clothes and a fresh towel through the slot after the breakfast tray. A sweater, underwear, and jogging pants with the drawstring removed. Three days was his best guess. They had been left to stew, probably to make them think.

Twitch closed his eyes tight. This was a nightmare. It had to be. From the smell and the cold, he guessed they were underground, probably under the International Mage Guild's obscenely expensive headquarters building. The damp made him feel cold constantly. There had been rumours about as much of the building being above ground as below it, but he had never come close enough to the building to verify this. The IMG was notoriously closed off to non-members.

With some time to mull over things, he had realised the IMG had gotten lucky. It was probably their plan to come in after them and hunt for clues, but instead they had found the entire party knocked out. The raid had taken mere minutes at that point.

Nothing they could have done could have avoided this. At least so he tried to tell himself, but his mind did not let him believe it.

What kind of idiot managed to spring a magic trap? He should have known but they had been in such a hurry to get the last book! The trap had not been described anywhere, and he had not checked properly. He had been distracted and now they were all in trouble for it. On a good day, he would have seen the trap from miles away.

He replayed the moment he lifted the book in his mind's eye, playing over and over. Though he had suspected the IMG of putting in the spell at first, they would have had no idea where it was to begin with. It had to have been some kind of spell Etta put in to keep it safe. It was fitting - if you were going to use this spell you had best prepare for some pain. But why had they been held for so long?

Perhaps they needed them to finish up the spell.

It was worrying. Hopefully by now the Elites would have noticed Furcifer's disappearance. And hopefully, Furcifer had told them where they were going. Gabrielle was a force to be reckoned with.

The situation was pretty grim. The sound of the opening door made him look up.

"He needs to use your shower." Said the man at the door. A younger looking man - the easiest to be bossed around, with the bravado to do the dirty work. Probably not very intelligent.

"Mine broke. It's so gross you shove us in here!" Furcifer huffed, but the man had already closed and locked the door behind him.

The mage looked exhausted, his hair frizzing from the humidity and lack of care. Furcifer held his towel tight. Though he looked confident, Twitch could see his nails had been bitten down to the nail bed.

"Right. They'll probably figure out I sabotaged my shower, but they won't drag me out of here mid washing up." Furcifer walked to the bathroom and turned the tap to warm the water.

"What are they planning?" Twitch whispered as he followed him and sighed. "Leave the door open. I want to talk."

"You pervert." Furcifer made a face and left the door open.

"You're the one who sabotaged your shower to get here."

"I'm well aware." He stripped out of his sweat pants. "This fabric is horrendous!"

"Hey, focus. What's going on?" Twitch snapped his fingers. It was the first time in days he had seen anyone.

"They want us to test the ritual. They've left us here so that they can solve all the issues with the Spell." Furcifer said. "Some of Ethan's mages came down to the cell and told me. I haven't seen Manon or Rebecca." It was clear he worried about the youths, especially Manon.

Twitch swallowed. "Quentin. The leader. He always wanted to resurrect Redford –."

Furcifer sighed. “With the death count on the spell, they'll want us to do the dirty work.”
“Sounds about right.” Twitch nodded, not liking that at all.

Furcifer stepped into the shower and looked over. “Tell me, is there anyway we can make this spell fail?”
“The spell will fail.” Twitch rubbed his face. “I've - I was preparing to use the spell. There is no way you can do this without some serious magic work before death.” He shook his head.

“Maybe we should not tell them that. Let them believe we can resurrect the man.” He peeked out before diving into the stream of water.

Twitch chuckled. “I'd call that morbid but we're discussing bringing back a wizard leader from the dead. Have you spoken to anyone else?”
“The ones I've spoken to are ok. Gabrielle is pissed off and broke a guard's nose, Salem is scheming.”
“Wait, they brought in Gabrielle?”
“Without Ethan, it's likely they want her in his place. Seven people, right? That's what the letter said.”

Twitch shivered. “In that case they probably still have Rebecca and Manon as well. Lydia?”
“She’s been trying to get them to call the embassy.” He said. “She’s handling it well. And I’m guessing the school will report the both of you missing.”
“Last time I was missing from a school I had to save myself.” Twitch shook his head and was unable to help the bit of anger that came up with.

His escape from the Scribes building had been... extraordinary. Pure rage and frustration had taken over after he had learned an innocent in the museum case had died, and he had taken down the entire building.
“I could use some of that Twitch now.” Said Furcifer, angrily rubbing shampoo into his hair. “Ugh! You don't have conditioner either?”

Twitch couldn’t help but laugh, and hand the man his towel. Furcifer dabbed at his eyes and blinked.
“Thanks for the updates.” Twitch nodded, keeping his eyes away from the man’s form.

"It's fine. I know you're worried about Lydia."
"I got her into this damn mess."
"And I got Gabrielle into this. I doubt she'll ever let that go.
"I wouldn't either, though."
"Wow, you should just apply for her job, you're just as merciless." Furcifer raised an eyebrow and dabbed his eyes before grabbing the soap.

"Well maybe I will." He looked over. "I mean, how hard can it be?" He asked.
"Very very hard!" Furcifer huffed.
"You've managed." Twitch looked over. "Didn't I remember you telling, nay, arguing with Gabrielle you don't like the job."
"But it's my job!" Furcifer looked out of the shower. "Ugh!" He washed his arms and rinsed off. "I still care for the Elites. I just... find it hard to study when people constantly asking for my help."
"So you don't want the job... But you want the job? I think you're just worried you'll lose your status. You wouldn't get so many spell books gifted to you. Youngsters wouldn't be flocking to you with their new spells hoping to get funding and or membership to get into the Elites."
Furcifer sighed and turned off the shower. "I'm done." He

said. "I'll be back tomorrow if I can play this ruse again. We will find a way."He started towelling off and put the tracksuit on again.
"Terrible fabric this is. So scratchy!"
"They provided underwear you know."
"I wear silk, not this... tarp!" Huffed Furcifer. "But we'll get out of here. I promise. For now, just do what they want. Even if it involves this... spell."

Twitch swallowed and looked over. He jumped a little as the young mage from before knocked at the door.
Surprising the man even bothered to knock, thought Twitch.
"Thank you, Furcifer." He said softly. This helped. Maybe Furcifer and he could think up a way to stop this.

The door opened and he looked into the face of a different young mage.
"Quentin is ready for you."

Chapter 46

They were lead into an enormous hall. From the lack of windows Twitch could tell they were still underground - but that was not what had drawn his attention the most. In the middle of the room was a large stone slab, as if for a sacrifice. Upon it lay a black body bag, strangely modern against the antique carvings of the altar. Furcifer's hair was still wet, and he saw the man shivering briefly in the cold room.

One by one the others were brought in, each with a young mage on their tail to guard them. Gabrielle pulled her arm away from the one walking her in as she was walked in last.

"I said get your hands off!" She bit. The guard took a step back, apparently easily intimidated. Twitch looked away. Seeing her here was probably the worst of it. He kept an eye out for Lydia.

Lydia rushed over to Twitch's side. "What's going on?" She whispered.

Quentin entered and motioned for the doors to be closed.

"Ladies, gentlemen." He looked around - all in all it was the seven of them, their guards, him, and whatever body was in that bag. Twitch shook his head. Very likely, it was Redford.

They would be resurrecting the leader of the IMG.

"I can see from your grave faces you all know why you are here. You've been chosen."

Quentin smiled brightly. "But I would like to reassure you, you are all safe here. This room has been adapted for this purpose." He put a hand on one of the pillars. "These pillars were enchanted by me, to attract and confuse any wayward spirits who come through that barrier. We wouldn't want to resurrect the wrong spirit."

"You're sick!" Lydia called out.

"Ah! Our transcontinental guest. Lovely to have you here." Quentin bowed to her. "I hope after this ritual and your subsequent release from here, you'll be able to enjoy America for a bit."

"You're letting us go?" Salem cocked his head.

"I can't very well kill you." Quentin looked to Salem. "You are... so prized. A mage with your wisdom... And with your gift I'm not even sure I'd be able to kill you." He looked around.

"No, nobody will die here by our hands. I merely ask of you that you perform the ritual, after which you will be turned loose."

Twitch cocked his head. They were laying on the sweet schmoozing - something that would probably convince Furcifer, but he was not so sure about the rest.

"But what if we don't do this?" Furcifer asked.

"Mr Furcifer. As a fellow leader you know we sometimes need to ask people to do the unpleasant. I really just hope you can cooperate. Because if you don't..."

"You'll kill us?" Furcifer raised an eyebrow.

"Yes. It'll provide excellent training on doing the spell." He said. "And the remaining people of your team might still be willing to do it."

A wheeled cart filled with books was pushed inside.
"All you will need for this ritual. The yellow books contain the spell and the ritual steps to take." He proclaimed. "The herbs will be coming soon."
Twitch picked up one of the books, almost dizzy as he read through the lines.
"He's right." He said hoarsely. His head spun even more as he recognised his own writing style in part of the spell. They had reconstructed the entire thing, undoubtedly by raiding their hideouts and houses to find the missing books.

This was a nightmare. It had to end. There was no way... He fell to his behind and gasped in a breath. He tried to dispel the dizziness by closing his eyes tight.

"I'm glad I managed to impress you, mr Ward." Said Quentin.
"What if the spell does not work?" Asked Furcifer.
"Ah! Yes. You're intelligent people. Why not... botch the spell and get off. It didn't work, too bad, so sad, better scrap all of this..." He laughed. "I took the liberty of providing you with an incentive." He walked over to the body bag and zipped it open.

This was not Redford, Twitch realised immediately. It was Ethan, apparently frozen as soon as they had found him. They had the cryogenic capabilities after all.
"I brought along Ethan. Your poor brother."
Lydia hissed. "You bastard! You let that man...!"
Quentin smiled serenely and finished zipping open the body bag. Something in that smile was inherently repulsive to Twitch. His casual behaviour only made him angrier. More determined.

"This is what I'm offering you. For us, it will be a test run of the spell and this room. For you, a chance to bring back your brother."
Twitch choked back a sob. Oh gods. He would have been happy to throw the ritual, maim a vowel here and there... But to get a chance to bring his brother back. He could not even think of it. He walked closer by, repressing his own disgust at the sight. He got up and put a hand on the pillar to keep himself upright.

He shivered. Back in the woods he would have been happy to destroy the book and leave it at that. He could have come to terms with Ethan's death, even the fact that it was his own fault. But to see him here made things horribly real.

"I'll give you and your group a few minutes to decide while I provide refreshments." Quentin motioned the mages out with him, but locked the door tightly.

"It's no use." Gabrielle looked around. "This room won't allow for any teleportation magic. We might just be sucked into one of those pillars."

Furcifer walked over. "Oh that is well done..." He sighed and studied the room further.

"We can still throw the ritual and get out. The fact he doesn't expect us to-"

"No!" Twitch laughed bitterly. "We don't even need to maim the Spell. It won't work either way."

"What?" Gabrielle looked over.

"It won't work. There needs to be preparation before death. You can't just do it on just anyone."

"How can I even believe you?" Furcifer growled.

Rebecca rubbed her eyes. "Guys! Stop it." She shook her head.

"Manon and me have lives to go back to. People who worry about us."

Twitch shivered, realising she was right. He looked around. Lydia was still calm, but how long would that last?

"What are the chances he knew the correct steps to take before all this?" Furcifer asked.

"He could have..." Twitch lit up. "He could have! He had access to the materials."

"Then I say we stall for time. First things first though. Neither

Manon nor Rebecca should be here."
Manon closed her eyes. "Rebecca knows who works with ... I mean worked with Ethan."
Furcifer nodded. "We ask for a trade. Have them ask Aiden here instead of Rebecca."
Twitch took a deep breath. Rebecca could find allies and have them rescued. The mages who had worked with Ethan were bound to be still around. Hopefully she could rally them.

Twitch nodded and calmed down. He couldn't imagine how worried Jeffrey would be about the man, considering he had lost a close friend to magic only a few years prior.
"Alright. I say we do this."
"I say we vote." Manon looked around. "Even if we don't do this, people will look for us, right?" She glanced around for agreement. "And we can think of ways to escape. If we do this, there is no turning back. They can... just do this for anyone. They could sell it for millions. Who knows who could come back all of a sudden! Tyrants could be revived. There would never ever be change."
"Do we need that? We're doing quite well. If we could keep the status quo..." Twitch was grasping at straws and he knew it.
"No, Twitch. You don't believe that." Salem shook his head.
"You and I have lived for so long, Salem! Are we so bad?"

Twitch whipped around to the other.
“No. But I can’t say it’s been pleasant.” Salem took a deep breath. “I would rather not do that to another being.”
“That’s right.” Gabrielle nodded. “Twitch. You stopped ageing. What if this is not just a resurrection, but a fountain of eternal youth?” She asked.
“I - maybe I age slowly. Maybe I just look good for my age.” Twitch said. “Look, how about we just take a vote?”

The mood in the room was tangible. Arms were being crossed but they did fall quiet.

“If you feel we should try and revive Ethan... And just revive Ethan. We can figure out what to do about the IMG having possession of this spell after that... Then raise your hand now.”
Twitch finished his sentence by letting his hand shoot up.

Salem sighed and put his hand up, as did Manon. After a few minutes, Furcifer put his hand up.
Gabrielle glared at him but put her hand up too. He hadn’t expected that, but it was welcome. They exchanged a curt nod, and he knew whatever debt she owed him for his mistreatment at her hands, it was now settled.
“What, I’m tempted to see how this spell works!” Furcifer protested as Rebecca groaned.
“That’s a majority. We’re doing it.” Twitch said.

"Wait." Rebecca sighed. "Look. This spell will affect all of us, even the ones against this... I'm not saying we shouldn't do it. I feel for your loss... But we need a better plan than risking our lives and then finding a way to steal the spell back."

Gabrielle nodded. "I agree." She said, looking over.

Lydia shivered. "I will participate as well." She bit her lip. "I'm... scared."

"It'll be alright." Twitch promised. "The magic in this room will help and we know what to expect."

At least he did - he had read the letter Ethan had managed to get to him, written by Henrietta. "But Rebecca is too young. She should not be here."

A murmur of agreement went up.

Lydia looked around and then sighed. "Sod it. I'm sick of that spell. But if I die I'm haunting you. You wouldn't want to bring me back." She joked shakily.

Twitch smiled a little. "Thank you." He took her hand.

It was another twenty minutes before the doors opened again. Twitch had briefed them on the ritual and was just explaining how it would happen.

"You've decided?"

"Yes, but on one condition." Said Twitch, taking the lead of the group. "We can't use Rebecca. Ask Aiden if he wants to

take her place. But she is too young."
Quentin nodded slowly. Behind him, the herbs were being brought in.
"Alright. I will let you write a letter. If he agrees to come, we will let Rebecca go. If he does not you will do it with the present company."
Furcifer nodded. "Let me. I know what might convince him."
Twitch nodded. It was a tall order to ask someone to risk their life for someone else.

Furcifer was handed pen and paper, and started writing. Twitch did not really want to know what he was writing.

☆☆☆

Aiden arrived an hour and ten minutes later.
"You came." Twitch was actually surprised.
Aiden nodded and looked to Furcifer. "He was... Convincing. Manon. Are you ok?"
Manon nodded, hugging Rebecca close. It seemed she was happy the other would be allowed to go free.
Quentin quickly moved between them and pulled Rebecca away.
"Alright. Brief your new team. You will start soon." Quentin looked around for any dissidence. But they were all too tired.

Aiden nodded and looked around. Manon wiped her face and looked to Twitch.
"How do we kick this off?" She asked hoarsely.
Lydia walked over and hugged her.

Twitch cleared his throat.
"So first, we share a meal. Then we draw the figures and spread the necessary herbs. The letter describes that Henrietta and her mages lowered the body into that circle but I doubt we can do that, so we just have to hope it works with the body present." It was somewhat similar to how they had found the spell.

Furcifer nodded. "I expect so. So then what?"
"We restore the body with the first chant. The second chant will be the hardest as it will open the... well, I guess it's a portal to the afterlife."
"The lethal part of the spell." Salem said, making Manon and Aiden recoil.
"Yes, but they warded against that - the souls who should not be here will go into those pillars. You can sense the strong magic. It will hold."
"So you think they did manage to make this ritual safe?" Furcifer asked.
"I wouldn't say safe, but I would say our odds are pretty good. We've had three days of good care to restore our strength - I

don't think that was just goodwill on their parts."
"So what after that? You think they will just let us go?" The hall was filling with sounds as a meal was being set out for them. Trays of catered sandwiches, fruit, pasta salad, and coffee and tea. It seemed so much like some sort of business lunch it was almost surreal, especially with the frozen body in the middle of the room. His head snapped back to the middle of the room as Quentin started talking again.

"Of course we will." Nodded Quentin. "What can you do to us?"
"Go to the police for kidnapping and... raising the dead!" Lydia called out.
"For one, kidnapping... Good one. But nobody here will testify you were held against your will. You were merely our guests! Nobody knew what happened in the forest. For all they care we rescued and fed hungry hikers. And raising the dead is still not an offense."
"You do know that if you do this, there will be a significant effect on your lifespan?" Aiden said softly. "I estimate everyone in this room will lose about five to ten years off of their life."

"And that's a sacrifice I'd be willing to make for my leader, given that it works." Quentin said. "And that's why you're going first. You should be grateful I'm giving you this chance to bring him back!"
"We wouldn't have to bring him back if you hadn't killed him!" Cried Twitch, before taking a deep breath.
"Fuck." He sat down. Aiden was right. All of them would live shorter lives.

"I can't order you to do this. I'm not a leader." Twitch looked around. "But who of you would be willing to do this with me?"
Try was more like it. If it didn't work though, he wondered if they would still lose the life span.

It was more of a "for me" than a "with me", he realised. He was asking a lot of the ragtag group which had only been brought together recently.
Lydia looked over to Twitch and took his hand. "I'm with you." She nodded.
Aiden nodded. "He's your family. You would help me protect

my family, too." Again, that glance at Furcifer.
Furcifer shrugged. "I just want to see if this works. Gabrielle?"
"I owe you one." Shrugged Gabrielle. "We're doing this."
Manon groaned. "Well.... I don't like the shorter life bit but... I'd rather not go back to that cell."
Salem laughed. "I doubt it'll impact me. I'll help." He got up and wiped his hands on his pants.

"Then let's eat." Nodded Twitch, looking to the table.

Chapter 47

Once, Furcifer had had lunch with a man who had threatened him with a gun under the table of a very crowded restaurant. He had owed the man a million after messing up a commissioned spell and causing serious harm to the man's brother. Even now he remembered the tense mood in the restaurant where they had sat down to discuss compensation.

Right now he would give all he had to be in that restaurant again, rather than here. He looked around the table, seeing everyone struggle to finish even a minute amount of food. Twitch was trying to set an example by munching on a sandwich, though it was clear he was still nibbling on his first slice of bread. Furcifer sighed and scooped up some of the pasta salad onto his paper plate. Tacky. If this was to be his last meal he –

No. It would not be his last meal. He looked around. The set up seemed solid, but it was clear that nobody was very happy about their odds. When the best case scenario was a shortened life span, it was hard to stay positive. The worst case scenario... He didn't even want to think about. The idea that he might not be leaving this room, that he would be dying in a cheap hoodie and sports... pants was horrible to him. He grabbed a cucumber sandwich. It tasted terrible and bland, but it was something. Right now he had to keep going. All this for a long shot, as well. But they had to stall for time. Once the IMG realised the spell would not work for them, all bets were off. They would no longer be safe.

He mentally went over the plan as Twitch had laid it out. Sharing the meal. Drawing the signs and the circles of protection. He had studied them, they were simple enough.
After that it was a matter of doing the first chant to restore the body, and then the actual revival. He shivered and quickly grabbed his cup of tea to wash down the cucumber sandwich.

Twitch was looking around. He looked a bit lost but he would hang in there until the end. Manon looked determined, probably aware that Rebecca would come speeding back with every soul she could find on her way up. Aiden, now he wasn't too eager but he had given him a large carrot, the name of Hayden's murderer. Now he just hoped the Witches hadn't been bluffing when they said they had it. Lydia was searching for another nail to bite, but at least it counted as getting food in. Salem... he was hard to read, but he was on Twitch's side. And Gabrielle, well, she was on his own side.

They still had no plan to get the Spell away from here but they could only do that once they had regained their freedom, anyway. For now their main priority was to remain safe. Remain alive. Pretend this spell would work. Honestly, he did not believe in it. Ethan had not seemed the type to aim for his own immortality. But he would be happy to be proven wrong.

He cleared his throat and dabbed his lips with a napkin.
"That was wonderful. Does everyone feel up to the next part of the Spell?"
The distraught looks he got were clear - nobody was really happy about this.

Twitch stood up. “Let’s do it.” He walked to the middle of the room and looked over the man on the altar for a second before breathing in deeply.
“Let’s do it.” He repeated.

Furcifer nodded.
“More spells, get your spells.” He tried to lighten the mood as he handed out all the papers. To see the IMG's logo on a spell that was basically his had to hurt.
Gabrielle rolled her eyes and grabbed the pages he was handing out.

“This is it huh? It looks so simple.” She shook her head and looked back up.
“I know.” Aiden looked over it. “I think this is the first time I’ve ever seen a spell so... elegant. It’s so simple, without fringes.”
“Too simple.” Furcifer sighed. “I think that’s why it cost so many lives... If it was just tweaked a bit.”
Quentin jumped up. “The Spell is ours now. We will tweak it where necessary.”
“Are you going to release it?” Aiden asked.
“Of course not. Internal use only.” Said Quentin.

Furcifer raised an eyebrow. It was only their word that said they would not be selling revivals to the highest bidder. For now. If times got hard again, even with their resurrected leader, perhaps they would turn to such things. It was clear they were going to have a hard time again at some point - they were using ridiculous, extreme solutions to solve things many organisations struggled with. Even he could see this kind of organisation could not last. Once the grandiose acts ran out, there was nothing that could be done and the guild would die a quiet death. And then, when someone went through the forgotten files...

Quentin looked around them. "I'll be outside with the other mages to avoid magic interference."
"You mean to avoid getting hurt." Manon interjected.
"You have one hour to perform the ritual. If it is not completed by then, we will destroy the body." He walked out, beckoning the guard mages who followed...
"Good luck." Quentin said, before closing the large door. It locked with a loud creak.

"We need to get started. This spell will run for about ten minutes and we still have to draw the symbols. Let's get to it!" Even if they were only pretending, he guessed Twitch wanted to keep up the facade... Or worse, did he actually believe this could work? He glanced over the shorter man. Even if Ethan came back from the dead, that was no guarantee of a happy ending for anyone in this room.

Aiden grabbed some chalk and looked over the drawings on the handouts.
"It's a protection circle with an inward allowance...." He nodded. "That's doable. What are the other symbols?" He pointed out some runic-style symbols marked inside and outside of the drawn circle.

"They're lucky charms, basically. Condensed luck spells, protection, health. Both for the ones performing the Spell as the one being brought back." Twitch looked over. "This will be helpful." He took one of the pieces of chalk and started drawing.

Salem looked over. “We can still stop, Twitch.”
“I’m not planning to.” Twitch replied, grabbing a piece of chalk to start drawing.
“Are you sure this is what Ethan would have wanted?”
“Ethan is dead. He doesn’t want anything.” Twitch angrily scratched a rune into the stone floor with the piece of chalk, which cracked under the pressure.
“It might not even work. So at least let me try.”

Furcifer sighed.
“All good, all good.” He grabbed another piece of chalk and started drawing as well. “As with any spell, we need our emotions neutral. We can’t let anger or fear control us now.”
Gabrielle nodded. “Furcifer is right. We need to be calm and collected when we do this.” Salem came to her aid and smiled a little.

“It’s all good. We’re doing this and it’ll go fine. Nobody will die.” Salem
“Easy for you to say.” Manon muttered.
Furcifer chuckled. “Glad you still haven’t changed.”
“Changed?”
“You’ve still got a big mouth.”
“Yeah, and be careful. I’ve learned to back it up.” Manon looked over with a little smile.

"We're ready for the first chant." Twitch said, after a check to see all symbols were in place.

Furcifer peeked over to make sure.

"It looks identical." He had to agree, tightening up a line on the main circle. It was an important one - if this one breached, even by accident, it could have grave consequences.

"Let's raise some hell." Furcifer looked over the page. Almost instinctively, everyone moved into a circle. And the first chant commenced.

Chapter 48

The chant reverberated through Twitch's chest, tapping into sources of magic he had not touched. He opened his eyes and saw his friends, similarly strained. It egged him on. As soon as the chant was done he staggered back to a seat, then grabbed a cup of coffee off of the refreshments table and downed it.

"Did it work?" He cleared his throat, realising he hadn't even checked Ethan's body.

"It did." Nodded Lydia. "He still looks dead. But... Freshly dead." She looked over to him and shivered. All of this had to be extremely unsettling for her, and he was immensely grateful she was still here with them.

"Thanks for staying." He said softly, walking back.

She looked up.

"I must admit this is quite scary. I did not think... I ever would... " She bit her lip.

He nodded. This was her first interaction with a faction. They were not making a great impression.

"Of course." He looked around. It seemed the mages were all exhausted after that. Manon was crouching, and Aiden hurled into a bin. The smell was... grounding, in a strange way.

"We'll take a few minutes." He looked at the clock. They had thirty five minutes left. It would be tight, but they could do it. He wiped some blood from his nose, hopefully before anyone could see it.

"The last chant takes twenty minutes to complete." Furcifer said. "We can't stop to rest now!"

"Yes, because one of us breaking down in the middle of the chant is so much better." Said Twitch. "I'm ordering you to take a few more minutes."

Had Furcifer forgotten their plan? He needed to stall for as long as possible. Or was he just swept up in the moment.

Furcifer growled but took an orange from the table, peeling it slowly and eating it angrily.

It was quiet. It seemed nobody was jumping to talk.

No wonder. After a few more minutes, Twitch got up and beckoned everyone close. Aiden wiped his mouth on a napkin, binned that and walked over.

Salem looked pale, but serene. He didn't seem to have any issue with this, though Twitch wondered if the man's life span would be impacted in the slightest.

"Alright. This is the scary part. The people who died during the spell - it was during this part. I suggest we move back to stand close to a pillar, or have a pillar between yourself and the altar where possible. Watch yourself." He took a deep breath as pages rustled.

"This is it." Twitch said, taking a deep breath before starting the spell.
Despite the electric lighting, it seemed the room was darkening. Before long the cause was visible - a portal was starting overhead. A dark, black vortex formed. Shadowy forms, preceded by primordial screams, flowed out of the portal and glared around. Almost immediately, one of the beings changed course and shot towards Twitch. He ducked and prayed, hoped for the best. Luckily, it was drawn in by the pillar next to him. Twitch let out a relieved sigh and glanced around for any signs of trouble.

So far, three of the shadowy beings had been sucked up by the pillars.
"Aiden!" Furcifer's voice rang out sharply, drawing Twitch's attention. It was hardly audible over the loud howling noise of the portal. This was magic that was not meant to be meddled with, Twitch realised, much too late. With a pang of terror he realised they could die, for real. Images of Lydia, dead, took over his mind. He closed his eyes tight and cleared his mind.

Aiden was walking towards one of the shadowy figures, and Manon, who was standing closest to him, was being stared down by a shadow. She looked too terrified to move and Twitch couldn't blame her. The shadowy figures were about seven feet, and looked like horrific ghosts. Most looked like decaying remains, covered by a thin veil of magic energy, white and glowing. Their presence was horrifying, wrong.

Furcifer slalomed between two of the figures towards Aiden.

"Aiden!"

"It's Hayden. Hayden is here. I sense her." Aiden said breathlessly. The shadow had grey eyes, much like the man's late wife. Aiden took a step forwards, in danger of being sucked away with the being. Even as a human being, touching such a strongly enchanted pillar was dangerous.

"No... Aiden. It's a trap. She would not lure you into danger." He shook his head. "Look away from her. Look at us. Remember what's real. Aiden!" He tried to get the man's attention. There was only a metre between him and the pillar now.

Aiden took a step forward towards the figure, but then shook his head.
"No! You're right. She's not – " He gasped and dove to the side, narrowly missing another shadow rushing towards him. This one had a familiar aura. She looked different from the others, her face mostly covered by thick auburn hair.

The second shadow veered away from Aiden, barrelling towards the interloper which had been luring him in. The auburn haired shadow tackled the other spirit, and rushed it back towards the portal, struggling with it before shoving it back in. The portal was a chaotic dark hole, but the auburn spirit paused and looked back. She stretched out a hand to Aiden but was pulled back in. As she vanished, Aiden cried out.
Furcifer blinked. From his angle he had seen it. Her hair had moved away from her eyes. Her grey eyes. The eyes he knew very well as those of Hayden Willemeens.

The sound was dying down, and the portal was closing. Spirits frantically tried to find an exit, but most were sucked into the pillars. Twitch could not imagine their fate. With a loud gurgling noise, the portal closed. At last, the quiet returned. After all of this, it felt more deafening than any spell.

"Is everyone okay?" Twitch called out.

With a gasp, Manon fell onto her behind. "Yes. I'm fine."

"I'm okay." Salem waved.

Lydia nodded. "Still alive." She rushed over to Manon.

Gabrielle waved her hand, sitting down near Furcifer. "Me and the ass are fine."

"Your ass is fine." Furcifer agreed. "I'm alive. Aiden's..."

"Aiden's okay." It sounded silently, almost hesitantly. Aiden cleared his throat.

"I'm fine. But that was her - that was Hayden. She went back into the portal, didn't fall for the traps. She saved another soul from being stuck in these pillars. It was her!" He raised his voice and wiped a trail of tears away, angrily. "She saved me."

Twitch bit his lip. "It's very likely that it was." He agreed, looking over. "I am so so sorry."

Aiden buried his face in his hands. Twitch understood why - this was the second time he had been unable to say goodbye to his wife.

Furcifer sat down by Aiden. "Twitch. Check on Ethan." He nodded to the altar.

Twitch blinked, but then rushed over. A glimpse at the clock told him they only had a few seconds left. Damn! He gently patted the man's cheeks.
"Ethan? Ethan, are you there?" What was one to say to check if one had come back from the dead? He shook him gently.
"Still nothing." He sighed. The body was slightly luke warm, but that might have just been because of the room's temperature.

A few more vigorous pokes and prods had little effect as well. Ethan stayed silent.

The door swung open. "Time's up."
"No!" Twitch glared up at Quentin. "We did it. We did it all like we were supposed to! It should have worked."
"So you say!" Bit the man, walking over to the man and checking his pulse. "No pulse. Back to your cells." He motioned for the young mages to come back. Twitch was the first to be grabbed, by a burly man who tried to wrestle him off of Ethan.
Twitch easily escaped his grip by using his full weight downwards, and rushed back to Ethan.

"No! No no no no!" Twitch pulled loose and rushed to the altar. "Come on Ethan. If I did it you're more than capable!" He said, shaking the man's shoulders and clinging to him.
"Kill him first. I'm tired of this little shit." Quentin said. Twitch wondered what he meant until he felt strong arms around his neck, pulling him against the burly mage's chest.
Quentin took a gun out of a holster and cocked it.
"But perhaps I should kill your girlfriend first."
Twitch was paralysed. He could not even see clearly - it seemed his eyes just refused to work.

Somewhere an alarm went off. A fire alarm? Quentin raised his arm, Lydia screamed. It shouldn't take this long. Time seemed to slow down. A shot rang from the open door, and he rolled off of the altar just in time.
"Lydia!" He rushed, staggered over to her, but she was upright, standing.

Quentin sagged down and the burly mage from earlier jumped over the altar for protection.
"It's me, let's go!" Rebecca called from the doorway. A few armed mages were flanking her. "The police will be here soon. We have to go now!" She rushed over to check on Manon and looked to the door.

Twitch glanced over to the body once more. Ethan was dead. With a shiver he walked over to Lydia and held her close. Was he crying? He wiped at his tears and let Furcifer lead him out the door. The copper smell of Quentin's blood spread as he crumpled, lifelessly.

It was over. Twitch knew, somehow, that there was no life in the man.

Epilogue

"It's a nice day huh?" Twitch tried carefully as he looked over Etta. She laughed bitterly and sat back in her chair.
"I guess so." She closed her eyes. "Where is that Gabrielle? If she wants to put me up in a nice flat I may actually take her up on it now. Wouldn't hurt to have some familiar faces around." She smiled weakly. The house was looking awfully big right now.
"I'll see what I can do. She's a little tied up right now." Twitch opened the fridge. Lydia smiled a little at the older lady and looked around for a seat, deciding on the love seat near the old lady's chair.

He brought a beer over to Etta's table, along with a beer for Lydia and a lemonade for himself.

It had been three months since their ordeal. The shooting at the IMG had been covered and the trial was still ongoing, though the mage who had shot Quentin had a good defense lawyer, paid for by Furcifer personally. They had tried to resuscitate Quentin on the scene, but to no avail. Twitch tried to forget everything he had seen that day, but he was called upon to testify, like most people in that room had.

Furcifer and Gabrielle had been cleared of all charges, if only because Twitch had not wanted to press any charges for things that had happened years ago. It was time to move on.

"I hear their new building is very airy." Lydia nodded. "And close to the beach, if only to ogle the guys."

"I like her!" Etta grabbed her beer. "You made a good choice bringing her over to meet me. She's a delight."

"I try my best." Lydia raised her beer.

Twitch smiled. Most of the reason had been that he knew she needed something positive after hearing about Ethan's death. They'd spent more time together, processing the loss. That first time he had come around to tell her the news... They had cried together. It had felt like the first time he had really been able to give his emotions free reign and it had been just what he needed.

"So what's going on with them International..." She made a hand gesture. "Come on, spill the beans."
"Well, they disbanded." He cleared his throat. "They were in debt after the whole quest and their building was seized when the trial started. Lots of bad magic in that place."
"You don't know the half of it." She said somberly. "I'm glad it's gone." She bit her lip and sipped some beer, staring outside.
"Lydia, are you thinking of joining any factions?" She asked.
Lydia hesitated and stroked Twitch's hand. "I don't think so." She said and looked over. "From what I hear they're kind of crap."

Twitch laughed a little and shook his head. They had cost him so much in the end, and it felt even more painful in the silence between them.
"You think of him often don't you?"
"He was my son. And the fact that... They almost killed both my sons... It weighs heavy, sweetie." She set the bottle down.

“Where is the spell now?” She asked.

“Destroyed. Furcifer had the mental presence to grab all of it before the police came. He had one of his technomages go through all of the hard drives we bought from the place after they shut down. Nothing of it remains. Not even my diary.”

“I had hopes you wouldn't find out, my child.” She sighed and looked down at the beer.

“You had a second chance and you - after you got used to life you just took it. You ran with it and made it your own. And me and Ethan are so proud of you. I just know.” She took his hand.

“I'm sorry I couldn't bring him back.” He squeezed her hand, biting back tears. “It's so unfair.”

“It is. But he protected what he cared for and in the end I know that was what mattered to him.” Etta said, as Lydia wisely gave them some room.

“She is a good one for you, by the way.” Said Etta, clearing her throat. “I think you should show the girl around America a bit.”

Twitch chuckled. “I will, but we came to see you you know.” He sat back. It was still heavy on both their hearts. They'd been talking a lot over letters until Twitch decided to at last make the trip over.

"I'm glad you came." Said Etta."Whatever happened... I'm glad it's been laid to rest." Twitch took her hand and nodded.

"I am too." He said.

Vade Mecum Series

Furcifer's Pride

Asa's Blessing

Coming Soon

Kaoru's Chaos